Alison Roberts is a New Zealander, currently lucky enough to be living in the South of France. She is also lucky enough to write for the Mills & Boon Medical Romance line. A primary school teacher in a former life, she is now a qualified paramedic. She loves to travel and dance, drink champagne, and spend time with her daughter and her friends.

THEIR NEWBORN BABY GIFT

ALISON ROBERTS

MILLS & BOON

Published in Great Britain 2018
by Mills & Boon, an imprint of HarperCollins*Publishers*
1 London Bridge Street, London, SE1 9GF

© 2018 Harlequin Books S.A.

Special thanks and acknowledgement are given to Alison Roberts
for her contribution to the Hope Children's Hospital series.

ISBN: 978-0-263-07724-7

MIX
Paper from
responsible sources
FSC C007454

This book is produced from independently certified FSC™ paper
to ensure responsible forest management.
For more information visit www.harpercollins.co.uk/green.

Printed and bound in Great Britain
by CPI Group (UK) Ltd, Croydon, CR0 4YY

CHAPTER ONE

THERE WERE TIMES when Evie Cooper wished she could clone herself, and this was definitely one of them.

As if it wasn't enough that she felt responsible for the success of this evening's gala opening for the Hope Children's Hospital, she was getting bombarded by seemingly urgent text messages from home.

Have you picked up the new test sticks for my blood sugar monitor?

She texted back to her father.

Yes. But I won't be home till late tonight. Have you got any left?

Think I've got one.

Evie briefly considered sending a message that, next time, it might be a good idea to let her know sooner that he was running out but she was distracted by her colleague, Michelle, who was looking flustered.

'The caterers have arrived. They're asking for you.'

'Tell them to get set up in the conference room. I'll get there when I've got a minute.'

Her phone beeped again.

Where are my skinny jeans?

She texted back.

No idea.

I put them in the wash DAYS ago! I have to wear them tonight for the school disco!!

Evie didn't respond. A couple of very anxious-looking people were approaching her reception desk.

'Welcome to ICU.' She smiled. 'You must be Mr and Mrs Taylor? Baby Cameron's grandparents?' She'd been warned they might turn up.

The man nodded. 'We're so worried about the little chap. We're hoping to get to see him.'

'I understand.' Evie nodded sympathetically. 'Let me see what I can do. Your daughter's in with him, of course, but it'll depend on how well he is whether anyone else can go into the unit.'

'But we're his grandparents.' The woman pressed a tissue to her nose. 'We *need* to see him.'

'I know.' Evie kept her smile in place. 'I understand completely. But we have a lot of very sick babies in our Neonatal intensive care unit and we have to make sure our staff aren't distracted in any way from doing their job. Please, take a seat in the waiting area. I'll talk to the doctor who's looking after Cameron.'

She put her phone on silent as it beeped again in her pocket. Her sister was fourteen now, for heaven's sake, not five years old—as she had been when their mother had died. Evie had too many other things to sort right now. Stella was old enough to sort her own laundry.

It took some diplomacy to appease the Taylors and it was Evie who came up with the idea of Cameron's mother taking a photograph of her premature baby and then coming out to the waiting area to talk to her parents-in-law for a few minutes.

Surely things would settle down now, long enough for Evie to dash over to the other wing of the hospital? As the head of the committee organising the gala function tonight, she wanted to make sure that the decorations in the conference room had been completed and that there were not going to be any last-minute glitches. What if the time-lapse video that had captured every stage of building this amazing new hospital wasn't already installed in the data projector, for example?

But Michelle was looking wide-eyed enough to suggest that something major had cropped up.

'There's people here from *Chat Zone*,' she whispered.

Evie frowned. 'I have no idea what you're talking about.'

'It's the society magazine that's giving all the others a run for their money. They're covering the gala tonight. Someone at main Reception has pointed them in your direction.'

'Why?'

'I don't know.' Michelle grinned. 'Maybe because

you know so much about everything around here? Can you talk to them?'

'I haven't got time. We're expecting that new neonatal cardiac surgeon to arrive any minute. The Australian guy?'

'Ryan Walker.' Michelle nodded. 'I can look after him. And ICU Reception for you. Go on, it'll only take a few minutes and…and the photographer is pretty cute. And we don't want Hope Hospital to get a bad write-up, do we?'

Maybe Evie could kill two birds with one stone. Take the journalist and her photographer to the conference room and check out the decorations and everything else while they set themselves up to record one of the most glamorous evenings that would happen in Cambridge this year.

But that wasn't what this pair were after.

'We've got plenty of time to do the actual event,' a pretty blonde, who introduced herself as Pippa, assured her. 'What we want is more background. Especially for the high-profile parts of the hospital like the neonatal intensive care unit.'

They both looked no older than her brother, Peter, who was in his last year of school. Evie suddenly felt a lot older than her twenty-eight years. She wanted to suggest that they could have done their homework in a more timely fashion. Instead, she drew in a deep breath and smiled.

'I haven't got long,' she warned. 'But I'll do what I can to help.'

Because that's what everybody expected of her,

wasn't it? And because that's what she did. Always had and probably always would.

'Can I get a shot inside the unit?' the photographer, Jason, asked. 'I've heard that it's a world-class facility.'

' ICU is actually two units,' Evie told him. 'It's a pod system, with PICU—that's paediatric intensive care—on one side and NICU—neonatal intensive care—on the other. They share a central staff station and service areas. There's room for growth with additional pods in the future if necessary.'

She took them as far as the entry-controlled glass doors so that Jason could get some pictures of the banks of monitoring equipment, the transparent, oval cribs and the incubators. The doctors here were wearing pale blue scrubs. The scrubs of the nurses and ancillary staff had a teddy bear print. Everybody was clearly focused on their tiny patients. Even at the central staff station, every patient was under direct observation or being carefully monitored via video cameras and data recordings from the wealth of the best equipment available.

'Every detail was chosen by our CEO, Theo Hawkwood.' Evie was so proud of these units. 'Even tiny things have had to meet the highest standards. Like all those windows to provide natural light and ceiling soffits and baffles to reduce echoed sounds. That paint colour on the walls? You wouldn't believe the amount of research that went into finding one that doesn't interfere with an observer's perception of skin colour.'

'I love the floor,' Pippa said. 'Those inserts in the wood look like rays of sunshine coming from the central station.'

'The flooring's state-of-the-art, as well. It has to absorb sound but also be good for infection control, maintenance and moving equipment. The inserts are aesthetic, of course. It is like a big sun, isn't it?'

'Only a private hospital with some serious financial backing could achieve something like this.' Pippa nodded. 'Mr Hawkwood's used his private fortune to build Hope Hospital, hasn't he?'

'It's certainly the realisation of a dream he's held for a long time,' Evie said smoothly. Not that she was about to start discussing her boss's personal business. 'But we don't simply take private patients. The mission of Hope Hospital includes pro bono cases and a focus on funding cutting-edge paediatric medical research that's going to benefit everybody. We also have some outstanding conference facilities which are going to attract collaboration from the best brains in the medical world.'

'His wife died, didn't she?' It was no surprise that someone from a society magazine would be more interested in a personal story than hospital architecture. 'I read that she got killed by a drunk driver, when she was out walking with their daughter, about five years ago. That's where the name Hope has come from, yes?'

Evie smiled. 'But it's also a wonderful name for a children's hospital, isn't it? If you came here with a really sick child, hope is the best gift we could give you. Mr Hawkwood hasn't just been involved with every detail of building this amazing hospital—he hand-picks the staff that get employed here, as well. People are coming from all over the world to join our team. We've got a new neonatal cardiac surgeon arriving

today, in fact, from Australia. Which reminds me...'
Evie glanced at her watch. 'I really need to check to see
if he's here yet. And get over to the conference centre.'

'We'll come with you.' Pippa smiled. 'But let's get
a quick shot of you out by the reception desk.'

'No...' Evie shook her head sharply. 'No photos of
me, please...'

Good grief. Imagine if a picture of her, in her plain
working outfit of this old skirt and jacket, got published alongside everyone in their gorgeous cocktail
dresses and tuxedos at the gala? And that was another
reminder. At some point, she had to find time to get
out to the car park, retrieve her dress and shoes and
do something to smarten herself up so that she could
attend the gala herself.

Michelle seemed happy to have a photograph taken.
She was still smiling as she handed Evie a handful of
paper notes.

'There's been lots of calls,' she told Evie. 'Sounds
like you're needed in the conference room. Mr Hawkwood is there already, I think.'

'I'm heading there right now. Has Mr Walker arrived?'

'No. No sign of him. No messages, either.' Michelle
looked unimpressed as she looked up at the clock on
the wall. 'It's getting late. Hey—don't you need to get
changed soon? You can't miss the gala.'

'Yeah... I'll get there.'

Hope Children's Hospital had been built with two
wings on either side of a round, central building that
had been publicly praised as an echo of Cambridge's
famous twelfth-century round church and it was po-

sitioned to be filled with natural light from walls of windows and for the upper floors to take advantage of the stunning views over the city of Cambridge. The intensive care units were on the top floor of the right wing, and the largest conference room was at the same level in the left wing.

It was already dark as Evie took her visitors across the top floor of the hospital, giving a rapid rundown of where other areas were located, like the theatre suites and wards, laboratories and research suites, but they seemed distracted.

'Look at that view,' Pippa breathed. 'You can see pretty much the whole of Cambridge.'

'Wait till you see the gala venue.'

Evie knew that the view from the glass wall of the huge conference venue would be breathtaking. The sparkle of the city's lights laid out below was going to be the perfect backdrop to tonight's event.

But Pippa wasn't thinking about the view when they arrived. 'That's Mr Hawkwood, isn't it?' She looked delighted. 'Do you think he'd have time for a quick interview?'

'I'll check. Stay here for a moment.' Evie eyed the long tables covered in crisp, white linen as she walked past. One was laden with champagne flutes that were gleaming under the lights and another was being set up with silver platters of delicious-looking finger food.

'Evie...' Theo Hawkwood was walking to meet her. Tall and charismatic, the former paediatric surgeon was so passionate about Hope Hospital, it was easy to forget how young he was to hold such a prestigious position. 'I'm so glad you're here. I wanted to thank you in person. I hear it's largely down to you that all this has come together.'

'It was a team effort, Theo.' Being in the spotlight made Evie feel distinctly uncomfortable. 'Everybody's worked very hard.'

'I don't know how you do it.' Theo smiled. 'On top of your job and those extra duties...'

Evie dismissed the question of how he knew about those 'extra duties'. This was his hospital and Theo had kept his finger on its pulse from the moment its doors had opened several months ago.

'I had a good training ground. My brothers and sisters were all very young when Mum died so I had to step up to control the chaos.'

It was an automatic gesture to touch the necklace she always wore when she thought of her mum. A gift to celebrate a wedding anniversary, her father had said he'd chosen the topaz stone because it reminded him of the colour of her mother's eyes. The hazel eyes that Evie had inherited. Heart-shaped and set in an antique-style gold filigree, Evie had worn the necklace every day since her mother had died. It had become her touchstone in those early years when she'd been trying to hold her family together.

Not that she'd been able to control everything, of course. Maybe keeping so busy now, all these years later, was a way of burying regrets—like having to give up her dream of being a nurse. She still got to work in a hospital and that was enough. Working in *this* hospital was a dream come true and she had Theo to thank for this opportunity. The flash of sympathy in his gaze reminded her that they'd both dealt with tragedy in their lives but he was the one who might have to deal with more memories than she would tonight.

'There's someone here from *Chat Zone*,' she warned him. 'The magazine?'

He nodded. 'I've heard of it.'

'They'd love to talk to you, but—just a heads-up—they might want to cover some personal ground.'

'Everything about Hope Hospital is personal to me,' Theo murmured. 'I'll talk to them. Briefly…our guests are starting to arrive.' He turned away. 'I'll see you later, of course.' A backward glance took in her outfit. 'You *are* coming, aren't you?'

'Just a couple of little things to sort first,' Evie assured him with a rueful smile. 'Like finding my dress.'

She avoided the group being offered a welcoming glass of champagne. She recognised Marco, one of their surgeons, and his department's boss, Alice, who was looking stunning in a sparkly blue dress. Naomi, a physiotherapist, was just behind them and the pale silk of her gown against her dark skin was so eye catching, it was no wonder that Jason already had his camera pointing in her direction. Evie sped towards the exit that would take her through the kitchen area. Luckily, checking that the caterers were happy was on her list of things to sort because she really didn't want anybody else to notice that she wasn't dressed remotely well enough to belong here.

Finally, thirty minutes later, she had the chance to do something about that. She hurried down the stairs, rather than wait for an elevator, out through the main reception area and into the chill of the autumn evening. Then she headed for the rear of the building, past the ambulance bay and the bank of huge wheelie bins for rubbish and into the car park where her practical little hatchback was close to the hospital end of the first row.

The pools of lighting here were designed for the safety of both vehicles and people so it was easy to spot the couple getting out of a car near to where she was heading. They were clearly going to the gala because the man was dressed in a tuxedo and the woman hanging off his arm was shimmering in a silver sheath dress, so low cut that Evie knew she had to be freezing. She was wearing silver stiletto heels as well and Evie had a moment of envy for anyone who could walk in heels like that. She'd tried it as a teenager—who wouldn't when you were only five feet two—but it had felt as ridiculous as trying to walk on stilts.

She could hear the woman giggling as the distance between them closed and she seemed slightly unsteady on her feet. Was it the shoes, or had this couple been enjoying a pre-gala drink somewhere? Her gaze shifted to the man, wondering if he was someone she knew, and then it caught in a flash of complete astonishment.

She didn't know him but he had to be the most gorgeous man she'd ever seen in her life. Even with his partner's choice of footwear, he was still a couple of inches taller than she was and the outer edge of the pool of light behind him seemed to have turned his hair into a tousled, golden halo.

He didn't notice Evie. Why would he when he had someone who looked like a supermodel leaning against him? They were so close now that she could smell the woman's perfume and hear her breathless request to be kissed.

'We're late enough already, Tiffany.' The man's voice had an edge of impatience and an accent that she couldn't quite place.

'No...' The woman tried to step in front of him and wobbled on her heels. She flung an arm out to steady herself just as Evie stepped within range. As a solid object that could be pushed against, the woman saved herself from falling by shoving Evie. It was Evie who was sent flying and she landed hard on the cold asphalt.

'Oops... My bad...'

Evie could hear the woman giggling again as she pushed herself up on her elbow. Yep, she'd definitely had a drink or two already.

'I'm so sorry about that. Are you all right?'

It wasn't a feminine scent she could smell now. It was something very, very masculine. Subtle but powerful at the same time, like the strength she could feel in the hand that was around her arm, helping her to her feet. This man was in control. He was also...annoyed? No surprises there. He was about to be even later arriving at the gala, wasn't he?

'Thanks,' Evie muttered, pulling herself from his grasp. 'I'm fine.'

But he didn't release his hold on her arm immediately. His gaze was searching her face. 'You sure about that? You had quite a bump.'

It was the fright of the fall that had to be responsible for the way her heart was thumping right now, not the fact that an incredibly good-looking man was holding onto her and looking as if...as if he could see past any attempt to brush off what was now an acute embarrassment. She must have looked like a complete idiot sprawled on the ground in front of this glittering power couple who were off to rub shoulders with the medical elite of the district.

And she wasn't just dressed in her boring work clothes, she was now covered in grime, half her hair had escaped from the pins that held it in a tidy knot and she knew that she had a rip in her skirt because she'd felt it happening when she'd fallen. She felt like Cinderella and the wannabe princess was looking way more annoyed than her prince. She tugged at the man's other hand.

'We're late, darling,' she reminded him. 'And I want some more champagne.'

The demand, even the tug, hadn't broken the scrutiny the man was still giving Evie and this was suddenly more than embarrassing. She could feel colour rushing into her cheeks and she wrenched herself free of the touch that was now burning her arm.

'I'm fine,' she said again. 'Enjoy your evening.'

It wasn't far to her car. Evie opened the door, leaned in to pull out the bag that contained her dress and shoes but paused as she straightened, her attention caught by the car that was parked alongside.

Flashy. That was the only word for the low-slung bright red sports car, and she knew instantly who had arrived in this vehicle. Good grief…she could actually see the silver-sheathed woman in the passenger seat, probably with her hand on her chauffeur's knee, doing her best to distract the man with that intense, discomforting stare who would no doubt continue to concentrate on the road ahead. Until he was *ready* to play, that was…

They would be amongst the gathering at the gala, along with all the other polished, successful people associated with Hope Hospital. Even if she got changed and tidied up her hair, Evie was still going to feel out of place there. A Cinderella who had a slightly incompetent fairy godmother?

With a sigh, she dropped the bag back into the car.

Her job there was done. She really didn't want to go the gala now.

But she wasn't expected home until late, either, and that provided an unusual window of freedom.

Evie turned back towards the hospital buildings. She knew exactly where she wanted to be right now.

And who she wanted to be with.

CHAPTER TWO

MAYBE IT WAS the jet lag.

Or perhaps it was that his new life was not beginning quite as smoothly as he would have liked.

Ryan Walker arrived at Hope Children's Hospital's opening gala alone. His companion for this event had started to feel unwell by the time they'd entered the main building of the hospital. Ryan had offered to drive her back to her hotel but Tiffany had sobered up enough to be embarrassed about her behaviour and had insisted on calling a friend to collect her. It was with a sigh of relief that Ryan took an elevator to the top floor. He wouldn't have wanted to meet any of his new colleagues with an inebriated woman hanging onto his arm. It was embarrassing enough that she'd knocked over that cute little blonde in the car park.

He hoped that stranger *was* all right. Oddly, he found himself still thinking about her as he stood for a moment to observe the crowded event. Maybe it had been her petite size that had made him feel like she might need looking after. Or maybe it was the way she'd been so keen to get away from him given that Ryan wasn't used to women reacting that way to his attention. He'd taken a second glance as he'd left the car park, only to see her getting into the car next to where he'd parked his rental. A staff car parking area, so maybe he'd see her again somewhere and could apologise again?

He hoped so. In the meantime, he was here to introduce himself to as many people as he could and a good place to start was obviously the man who was in charge. It was lucky that he could recognise Theo Hawkwood so easily after the video call conversations they'd had. And how flattering had it been that he'd been headhunted to join the team of this new centre of excellence that was just getting off the ground?

'Theo...' Ryan extended his hand. 'It's so good to meet you in person, at last.'

'Ryan... So glad you could make it. I was hoping to give you a tour of the hospital today but it's been a bit crazy, thanks to this event.'

'No worries. My flight got held up in Singapore so I didn't have the chance to get here earlier. I'll look forward to a tour tomorrow. I've still got a day or two before my first theatre list, yes?'

'Of course. Come and find me first thing in the morning. In the meantime, let me introduce you to a few people.' Theo turned to the man next to him. 'Starting with Marco Ricci, one of our general paediatric surgeons. Marco, this is Ryan Walker, our new neonatal cardiac surgeon.'

'Delighted.' Marco shook Ryan's hand. 'Can I find you a drink?'

Ryan shook his head. He was still unimpressed with Tiffany's earlier behaviour. Who would have expected cabin crew to let their hair down quite that much on a night off? And, with that thought, he was reminded again of the woman who'd been knocked over. Not really blonde, exactly—more like a pale redhead. Different...

There were a lot of people who wanted to talk to Theo and Ryan found himself left with Marco.

'That's Alice Baxter.' Marco pointed out a slender woman with strikingly pale blonde hair. 'My boss.'

Ryan's eyebrows rose at something in his tone. 'Oh?' Good grief, this hospital had only been up and running for a short time. Were there politics going on already?

'She's bossy.' But Marco's smile was charming enough to suggest that this might not be a criticism. 'I'm waiting to find out if she'll loosen up a bit after a glass of champagne, perhaps.'

'So who else is here from the surgical team?'

'Hmm...' Marco looked around. 'Finn Morgan should be here, but it wouldn't surprise me if he isn't. I've never seen him at a social event.'

'Are there a lot of them?'

'Not really. But I'm sure there'll be more as we get closer to Christmas. So, what would you like to know about Hope Hospital?'

'Tell me about ICU,' Ryan said. 'I can do my best in Theatre but the standard of aftercare is obviously critical to the best outcome.'

'Oh, you'll be impressed. Come with me and I'll introduce you to the head of the department. She'll want to meet you, as well. I think I spotted her a while back, on the other side of the dance floor.'

Ryan followed Marco, smiling at people as they

nudged their way through the crowd and pausing to provide his name to a woman with a photographer who'd just snapped his picture. His work with children's charities made this a familiar environment and no doubt he'd be meeting some of these people again soon enough. He already had tickets to a charity ball in London in a few weeks' time. He was happy enough to be starting his new position with a party but what Ryan was really looking forward to was the peace and quiet of an operating theatre and being able to focus on what he did best.

Mending broken little hearts.

It felt peaceful already.

The main ICU reception area was not staffed at this time of night. Administration tasks could wait until normal working hours and visitors were restricted so Evie's work station was deserted and the lights dim.

That wasn't where she was heading, however. Behind Reception was a corridor that led to the staffroom, departmental library, overnight bedrooms, changing rooms and showers. She used her coded lanyard to gain access to the female changing rooms and paused by the shelves just inside the door, choosing her size in the teddy bear printed scrub trousers and tunic top. Getting changed, she realised just how bad the rip in her skirt was. Maybe she would ask Janine, the nurse manager who was on tonight, if it would be okay if she wore the scrubs home tonight.

Moving towards the mirrors, Evie found a hairbrush in her bag and dealt with the mess of her hair, brushing it smooth and then braiding it into a simple plait to hang halfway down her back. It was only as she looped the tie around the end of the braid that she realised what was odd about her reflection and she froze in horror.

Where was her necklace?

Her touchstone?

Desperately, Evie tried to think of where she might have lost it. Not long ago, that was certain, because she remembered the feel of it below her fingers when she'd been talking to Theo.

Her fingers were resting on bare skin now, the image of Theo in his tuxedo in her mind. Then she remembered another figure in a tux. Helping her up from the ground. That fall had done more than rip her skirt, obviously. Somehow the necklace must have caught and the chain had been broken.

Evie breathed out slowly, resisting the impulse to change back out of the scrubs and go looking for the necklace right now. It was a staff car park and the only value of the jewellery was sentimental so if someone found it, surely they would hand it in to the main reception desk? And if nobody had noticed it in the dark, which was more likely, it would still be there when she went back to her car.

This time was precious, too, because it was Evie's favourite thing in the world to do and she knew that others appreciated her efforts.

She was good at it, as well.

Janine gave her a smile of welcome that made her feel special as she buzzed herself through the main doors of the ICU.

'It's our baby whisperer. No way... I was just saying that it was a shame you were busy at the gala tonight.'

'I decided I'd rather do some cuddling. Is that okay?'

'Are you kidding? You must have known you were needed. Baby Alfie's mum had to go home to the rest of the kids and he just won't settle. Come right this way...'

Beside each oval crib or incubator here was a comfortable chair with a padded seat and back but designed to look like an old-fashioned rocking chair, complete with rockers. It was a distinctive touch that added to the unique atmosphere of this high-tech unit, rather like the sun rays set into the flooring, and it was much loved by the stressed parents who spent time with their babies here. Staff rarely had the time to sit for long to comfort the tiny patients whose parents couldn't be here and Alfie was a prime example. Born early enough to need his breathing carefully monitored but not in need of any major interventions, his distressed whimpering had not been silenced by ventilation tubes or sedation and all he really needed at the moment was a cuddle.

Evie settled herself in the chair and Janine took the tiny bundle, swaddled in a blanket with a woolly hat on his head, and put him into Evie's arms.

'He's been fed and changed recently so he just needs to sleep,' Janine whispered. 'Work your magic, Evie.'

The magic needed to work both ways tonight, Evie thought, stroking the tiny screwed-up face with a gentle finger.

'Shh...shh...shh...it's okay, Alfie... Everything's okay...'

She cradled the baby, rocking slowly in the chair and making soft, soothing and often nonsensical conversation with this tiny person.

Around her, staff members worked quietly with the

more serious cases under their care. A doctor came for one of them and Evie noticed an incubator being wheeled away, probably to the procedures room. She sent silent good wishes along with the entourage.

The beeping of the equipment was muted, voices were kept low and the lighting was as dim as it could be to still allow staff to work. Alfie's whimpering was already becoming just the occasional snuffle and squeak and Evie closed her eyes, aware of nothing more than the weight and warmth of this precious bundle.

It was a kind of meditation and she could actually feel her own heart rate and breathing slowing. The stress of an overly busy day, the never-ending pressure from her family, even the fright of that fall in the car park and that disconcertingly intense scrutiny that stranger had given her were receding as noticeably as an outgoing tide.

This was Evie's time.

But, like all good things, it had to end. Whatever crisis had occurred in the unit had been dealt with and Janine finally returned. Alfie had been sound asleep for a long time but Evie would have stayed there much longer if she could have.

'You need to go home.' Janine smiled. 'You've got work in the morning, remember? And Alfie needs to sleep on his apnoea mattress. Just in case.'

'Of course.' Evie's arms felt empty as Janine lifted the baby. 'Anyone else need a cuddle?'

Janine shook her head. 'Next time.'

Evie watched as Alfie was settled into the incubator and the monitors checked and then she followed Janine back to the central station.

'Would it be okay if I brought the scrubs back in the morning? I had a bit of an accident with my skirt and it's not really wearable.'

'Sure. No problem. And thanks, Evie. You were a real help tonight. I hope you don't regret not going to the gala.'

Evie shook her head. 'Things like that aren't really my thing, you know? I'm too much of a homebody.'

'You're a treasure,' Janine told her. 'Go home and sleep well.'

The delicious grounding that baby cuddling had provided took a hit as Evie went out into the cold night air. Her coat on over the borrowed scrubs, her work clothes stuffed into her shoulder bag, she walked into the car park with her head down, searching for a metallic glint against the asphalt.

How was she going to confess to her dad that she'd lost the treasured keepsake? Oh…and had she put that pack of blood glucose testing strips in her bag? Evie had to pause for a moment and fish under the wadded clothing to feel for the outline of the box in her bag. Her brain was jumping back into reality fast now. Was Stella home from her school disco yet? Had Bobby done his homework? Had *anybody* washed the dishes?

The box was there. With a sigh, Evie carried on but she knew the search was pointless. She was past the spot where she had fallen now. Almost at her car, in fact. Finally raising her gaze from ground level, she became instantly aware of two things.

The first was that the flashy red car was still parked alongside hers.

The second, and far more alarming thing, was that the man who presumably owned the car was leaning against it. Watching her.

Waiting for her?

And then Evie gasped as she noticed a third thing. Below the white cuffs at the bottom of the black sleeves of this man's tuxedo, something was dangling from his hand. A gold chain. A gold chain that had a heart-shaped topaz.

'I'm thinking this might be yours?'

He was smiling at her, but the generous curl of his lips didn't match that intense stare and Evie couldn't smile back.

Who *was* this man?

A complete stranger but she recognised something about him.

No. It was something she was recognising about herself. Heavens…had it been that long since she'd experienced a real physical attraction to anybody? So long, it took a moment to interpret that odd sensation that started deep in her belly and then spread like wildfire through her veins.

Any smile she might have dredged up was nowhere to be found now.

She'd felt like this once before, hadn't she? And look how well that had ended up. She'd kept herself safe ever since and that wasn't about to change now.

'It is, indeed,' she said, her tone clipped. 'I realised it must have broken when I…um…fell over.'

'When you were pushed over, you mean. I must apologise again. My…ah…companion was a bit over the limit.'

'Mmm…' Evie wasn't about to excuse the woman's behaviour. Where was she, anyway? A quick sideways glance told her that nobody was sitting in the car waiting for him.

'The least I can do is have it fixed for you.'

'No.' Evie stepped forward, her hand outstretched. 'That's really not necessary. But thanks for the offer.'

He seemed reluctant to let the necklace go so Evie had to try and take it from his hand. The instant her fingers touched his, however, the awareness of skin against skin was electric and she instinctively snatched her hand away again.

Wow… Now she remembered the way his grip on her arm had started to burn and that had been with a protective layer of clothing between them. That touch had been…had been like nothing she'd ever experienced before.

It had happened so fast it was no more than a slight hesitation but if she didn't cover it up just as fast, this was going to get awkward.

Okay…it was awkward already and it had only taken a heartbeat. Had he felt that jolt as well or was he just aware that *she* had. Why couldn't he just reach out himself and hand her the damn necklace?

Evie couldn't look up and meet his gaze. Because she knew he was staring at her and she also knew that he would be able to see exactly why she'd had to snatch her hand away.

He wasn't even saying anything to diffuse the weird tension that had sprung from nowhere.

It was only another tiny moment of time. Just

enough to suck in a single breath but the silence seemed charged.

And then it was broken.

Not by this man saying anything. Or Evie saying anything. Or the footfalls of anyone else arriving in the car park. It was broken by another sound. High-pitched and wobbly. Like a kitten mewing.

Except that Evie spent enough time around babies to think it was very unlikely to be a kitten.

'Did you hear that?' Her head turned so that she could look in the direction the sound had come from—that bank of wheelie bins tucked out of sight at the back of the hospital. The bin on the end was one of those wire mesh ones that took folded cardboard for recycling but someone hadn't bothered to squash one of the boxes and put it in the bin. This box was tucked between the recycling bin and a solid bin but it was poking out far enough to make it easily noticeable.

Another tiny mew cut through the still air and Evie turned her whole body now, her necklace completely forgotten. She was aware that the stranger was follow-ing her as she ran towards the box but it didn't matter. Any tension between them had been forgotten along with the necklace, in the face of something far more concerning.

Ryan dropped the necklace into his pocket with a sigh as he followed this suddenly rather irritating small woman.

He wanted to get to his bed and sleep off his jet lag so he could be on form for his first day on the new job tomorrow. When he'd spotted the glint of jewellery on the way back to his car, he'd known instantly that it probably belonged to her. It had been a surprise to find the car that he'd seen her open was still there, parked alongside his, so he'd been waiting and thinking about what to do. Take the necklace into Reception? Hang onto it in the hope of seeing her somewhere around the hospital? He'd certainly recognise her easily. He'd finally come up with the solution of tucking it under the windscreen wipers of her car when he'd seen her coming into the car park, her head bent as she walked slowly, clearly looking for her lost property.

Why hadn't he said anything? Or walked to meet her? What had been with that odd urge to simply watch her getting closer to him? To let the anticipation build until she noticed him and met his gaze?

And what on earth could explain that really weird moment when she'd touched his hand and jerked away as if it were a hot coal? He'd felt the heat, as well.

She was ahead of him so she reached the box first, crouching down beside it. She was wearing scrubs under her coat so he assumed she was a nurse at Hope Hospital and that was a pleasing thought. He'd probably see her again, then...

'Oh, my God...' She was peering into the box. 'I *knew* it had to be...'

'What?' Ryan crouched beside her. 'Good grief... a *baby*?' He lifted the box, moving to where he could catch some light from the nearest lamp. He didn't like the colour of the baby's face and it was clearly in some respiratory distress because it could barely summon the strength to cry. Without hesitating a moment longer, he began striding towards the back entrance of the hospital.

'Where are you going?' She was almost having to run to keep up with him.

'I need to examine this baby properly. It's not well.'

'*You* need to examine it?'

'I'm a doctor here. Or I will be tomorrow.' He kept moving. 'My name's Ryan Walker.'

'Oh… You're the new surgeon? The Australian?'

'Yep.' Ryan had reached the door. Unlike the main entrance, this one needed a security pass to open it from the outside.

'I'll do it. I've got a card.' She leaned past him. 'I'm Evie Cooper. I work here.'

'Where's the emergency department? Oh, I don't suppose there is one, with this being a private hospital?'

'I work in Intensive Care,' Evie told him. 'Let's take him there.'

Ryan nodded as he followed her inside. 'Lead the way. And let's hurry.'

CHAPTER THREE

JANINE LOOKED SHOCKED, as well she might, when Evie hurried into the neonatal intensive care unit accompanied by a man in a tuxedo who was carrying a cardboard box. One of the intensive care specialists, Susie, was sitting beside Janine at the central station and her jaw dropped as well.

'A baby's been abandoned in the car park,' Evie explained. 'A neonate.'

'I'll take him.' Susie was on her feet now.

'Procedure room?' Janine asked.

'I'd like to examine him myself,' Ryan told them. 'I don't think this baby is well. And I don't think it's simply hypothermia.'

Both the women behind the desk stared at him.

'This is Ryan Walker,' Evie said. 'Our new neonatal cardiac surgeon?'

'Oh...' Susie blinked. 'Pleased to meet you. You've been at the gala, I guess.'

'Yes.' Ryan's smile was tight. He clearly didn't want to waste time on introductions. 'Where is this procedure room?'

'Right this way.' Janine was back to her normal calm efficiency in the face of any emergency.

There was no real reason for Evie to go with them but nobody stopped her and she didn't even pause to think about whether it was appropriate. She was the one who'd heard this infant and discovered him. She was already involved. Connected. Worried sick, even.

'I'll get the heaters on,' Janine said, as soon as they entered the clinical space, which was equipped with everything they could possibly need, including ventilators and an empty, state-of-the-art incubator. 'Where did you find him? Just out in the open in the middle of the car park?'

'No. He was kind of hidden between the wheelie bins near the ambulance bay,' Evie said, and the squeeze around her heart was almost painful.

Ryan put the box down and then reached inside to carefully lift the baby out. It was wrapped in a piece of clothing as a blanket. A well-worn hoodie.

'It's a girl,' Susie murmured. 'And very recently born. Within the last hour or two, I'd say. Oh, my…is that a hair tie on the cord?'

'How long has she been outside, do you think?' Janine had switched on both overhead and mattress heaters. 'It's freezing out there.'

'It has to be more than half an hour,' Ryan said, stripping off his tuxedo jacket and throwing it into a corner of the room. He started to roll up his shirtsleeves, stepping towards the sink to wash his hands. 'I was standing not far away for at least that long and I would have seen somebody leaving the box.'

He turned his head to glance at Evie, which made

her blink and then catch her bottom lip between her teeth. He'd been standing in the car park for at least half an hour? Waiting for her so that he could return the necklace?

Wow…

It made her feel…special?

More than that…it reignited that sensation in her belly and gave her a disturbing flashback to that moment when her fingertips had touched his hand. This had to stop, right now. It was worse than simply finding a man attractive. This Ryan was a doctor and that put him completely out of her league even if she was prepared to consider getting close to someone. She'd been taught that lesson long ago. And she wasn't interested in getting close to anyone, anyway. So much safer not to.

But she couldn't look away from this someone, despite her best efforts. This was her first proper glimpse of the man in strong lighting and it stole her breath away. Tanned skin on muscled forearms was dusted with golden hair and there were matching streaks of gold on his head. He looked like someone who spent all his spare time on a beach, which was not unlikely given that he had come from Australia. Something like surfing was probably a normal hobby over there. He had blue eyes, she noticed as he turned back to the table. Very blue eyes…

With an actual, physical wrench, she dragged her gaze away from him. It snagged on the empty box that had been the baby's only shelter from the chilly autumn night. Except…it wasn't quite empty, was it?

'There's a note in the box,' Evie said.

Only Janine glanced in her direction. Ryan and Susie were completely focused on the baby, checking her out from head to toe.

'What does it say?'

'"Please help my baby. Find her a mum who can look after her because I can't."' Evie's voice choked up. 'It looks like it was written by a kid... Oh, I hope she's okay...'

'They'll find her,' Janine said. 'Or maybe she'll come back to find us.'

Evie swallowed. 'I don't know about that. How desperate would you have to be to leave your baby and run away?'

She put the note back with the box and the hoodie—the only items they had that might provide a clue to the mother's identity and perhaps her whereabouts. Where had she given birth? And had she been all alone? How frightening would that have been?

Evie took a step closer to the table where the doctors were examining the tiny baby. She was so tiny. Naked and vulnerable. She had stopped crying for the moment and, while her body was squirming under the attention of professional hands, her eyes seemed to be trying to focus on the nearest face—as if she was searching for someone she recognised.

'I can't see any obvious major abnormalities,' Susie said. 'But I'd only give her an Apgar score of about six. Seven at the most. Her respiratory effort is down and her colour's off. Look at her legs.'

Evie looked as well. While the baby's upper body was quite pink, her legs were very pale and the tiny toes had a distinctly bluish tinge.

'Differential cyanosis,' Ryan nodded. 'Let's check the peripheral pulses.'

His hands looked huge against the tiny body under the warmth of the lamps. Clever-looking hands, Evie thought, and so gentle as he felt for the different pulses. Brachial at the elbow, radial in the wrists and femoral in the groin.

Janine, standing close to Evie, let her breath out in a sigh. 'Poor little mite,' she murmured. Oh… I'd better call the police, hadn't I? And Social Services?'

'It can wait for a bit. I want to know what's going on here.' Ryan's face was creased with concentration and then his frown deepened. He put his fingers on the baby's chest, very softly, and he closed his eyes for a moment. Was he feeling for the way the heart was moving?

His eyes snapped open. 'Stethoscope?'

Susie pulled hers from around her neck and handed it to him. Evie caught the glance she gave Janine that suggested they might be lucky in having a cardiac specialist on hand.

'Femoral pulse is absent,' Ryan said, as he warmed the bell of the stethoscope in his hand. 'And the radial is weak.'

It had to be hard to hear any heart sounds with the warbling cries the baby was making again. Maybe that was why Ryan cupped the tiny head with one hand, his thumb offering a comforting stroke over the whorls of dark hair. Watching him do that melted something deep inside Evie, maybe because it was so tender and suggested a concern that went beyond anything purely professional. Then he nodded once and straightened and it was clear that his only thoughts were clinical.

'Systolic murmur,' he said.

'Congenital heart condition.' Susie nodded. 'What's your guess? A ventricular septal defect, maybe?'

'Could be. Or a hypoplastic left heart. Or coarctation of the aorta. We need to get some ECG dots on and do an ultrasound.' He looked down at the baby and his mouth curved in a poignant smile that made Evie's heart skip a beat on top of that melting sensation.

'You're having a bit of a rough start at this game of life, aren't you, sweetheart?'

'She needs a name,' Janine said. 'Even if it's just temporary.'

'Grace...'

Everybody's heads turned and Evie blushed. The name had just popped out before she'd stopped to think.

'It was my mum's name,' she added. And she'd been thinking of her mother just before she'd found the baby, hadn't she? Her mother's necklace, anyway.

'I like it,' Susie said. 'Grace it is.'

'Can she stay here?' Ryan asked. 'What's the protocol at Hope Hospital for treating abandoned babies?'

'I have no idea. It's not something you expect to happen, is it?' Janine shook her head. 'I'd better get hold of Theo and let him know what's happening. He might not have left the gala yet and he'd better be the one to handle police involvement and any media coverage, etcetera.'

'I could do that,' Evie offered.

'Oh, please do,' Janine said. 'You'll know all the

numbers needed. But don't you need to get home to the kids?'

'I'll call and make sure everything's good. And then I'll stay as long as I can.' Evie took one more look at the baby. She didn't want to leave.

What she really wanted to do was to pick up this baby and cuddle her—more than she'd ever wanted to cuddle any of the babies here.

She'd found this one. And she'd named her.

The feeling of connection was rapidly getting stronger.

Ryan seemed to sense her hesitation. 'Don't worry,' he said softly. 'We'll take good care of her while you're gone.'

As if to underline the promise, he touched baby Grace's hand with his forefinger and she saw the tiny fingers curl around his. That image stayed in her mind with startling clarity as she headed out to the reception area and the phones she needed to use.

There was so much to do to stabilise this baby's condition and the medical team was very busy for quite some time. Inserting an umbilical arterial catheter was always a challenge but delicate procedures with such small vessels were precisely what Ryan Walker was so good at.

'I'll take a sample of blood. Is there any way we can get an arterial blood gas measurement immediately?'

'Yes.' Susie took the syringe containing a tiny amount of blood. 'We've got a small lab here and I can run this one myself. If we need anything else, there'll be a technician on call all night.'

'I want to get a Foley catheter in as well, to monitor renal perfusion and urine output. And do we have a portable ultrasound?'

'Yes. Do you want me to call in an ultrasound technician?'

'No. I'll do it myself.'

'Do we need to put Grace on a ventilator?'

'Not yet. But we'll keep a close eye on her oxygen saturation levels. We'll need the go-ahead for any further invasive procedures, won't we?'

'Theo's on his way,' Janine told them. 'He's with the police at the moment. And the security team. They're having a look at the CCTV footage that covers the car park area.'

Theo Hawkwood arrived as Ryan was completing his ultrasound examination.

'Are you okay to be doing this?' he asked Ryan. 'It's a bit of an unexpected start, isn't it? How's the jet lag?'

'No problem,' Ryan assured him. He had forgotten he'd even been weary, in fact, faced by the adrenaline rush of this case.

'What are we dealing with?'

'Looks like quite a severe coarctation of the aorta. Along with a ventricular septal defect, although I don't think that's overly significant.'

'She'll need surgery?'

'Possibly. We'll start some medication and I'd like to do an angiographic study as soon as possible, when we've got a full team available for the catheter laboratory. I could do a balloon angioplasty as well, which would be a bridge to surgery, if it wasn't enough by itself. Unless...' Ryan looked up to meet Theo's gaze.

'Can we treat her here or do we need to transfer her to a public hospital?'

Theo shook his head. 'We're set up to take a percentage of pro bono cases. Someone has entrusted her to our care and I want Hope Hospital to do everything possible to help.'

'What did the police say?'

'They've got the CCTV footage. We can't get a good look at the girl's face but it's a start. And they think there must be other people that will know something. She couldn't have given birth entirely by herself, surely?'

'It's not an unlikely scenario,' Janine said. 'Especially if the girl was hiding her pregnancy. Poor thing,' she added. 'I can't think of anything worse.'

'The police are out in the waiting area at the moment. They want the box and any other evidence that might help. I understand there's a note?'

'Yes. It doesn't say much. Just that the mother isn't able to care for the baby.'

Theo nodded. 'Someone from Social Services is coming as well. They're going to take care of registering the baby and signing her over to our care for now.'

'We've given her a name,' Janine told him. 'Grace.'

He smiled. 'Nice. I like it. A name with meaning. Like my Hope.'

'Your Hope?' Ryan raised an eyebrow. 'You mean this hospital?'

'It was the name of my wife,' Theo said quietly. 'And building this hospital had been a dream for both of us.'

'Grace was Evie's choice,' Susie said. 'Apparently it was her mum's name.'

Ryan was watching Grace's ECG trace on the monitor screen again. Evie hadn't hesitated to offer that name for this baby. The memory of her mother had to be very strong. He'd noticed the way she'd been watching the baby during their assessment of her, too. Did she always bond with her patients so completely? Or maybe it was because she was a mother herself? Hadn't someone said something about her having kids at home?

She hadn't wanted to leave the room, either. Oddly, despite his total focus on everything that still needed to be done after that, he'd also noticed her absence. There was certainly something about her that was different, and it wasn't just her unusual hair colour. Something that interested him. She was completely off limits, though. That comment about her having kids at home had been a red flag. A whole ring of red flags, in fact, that had her penned in its centre. Women who wanted kids were enough of a problem. One who already had them was someone who inhabited a planet Ryan was never going to visit.

Somehow, he wasn't surprised to find her out in the unit's reception area, when they'd finally settled baby Grace into a space where she could be monitored continuously until the catheter laboratory was available first thing in the morning. He'd been offered one of the overnight rooms here and he had to pass the reception area on his way to find it.

'You're still here,' he said to Evie. 'You're not actually on duty, are you? You must have been on your way home when I met you in the car park?'

She nodded. 'I was just waiting. To hear an update on Grace...'

The weariness that had been banished by the need for action had come back with a vengeance but Ryan pushed it aside as he pulled out a chair to sit down beside Evie.

He'd seen many faces that looked like this but only on parents who were waiting for news on their sick babies. Desperate faces that could make it very hard to stay professionally distant but that was another one of Ryan's skills and he knew exactly how to deal with it. By providing whatever information he could and being very honest about his opinions without letting emotion cloud any issues.

'Grace has a coarctation of her aorta.' He could see that his words hadn't triggered any more than superficial recognition. Was Evie only a junior nurse, perhaps? 'It's a narrowing of the main blood vessel that comes from the heart,' he added.

'Sounds serious.' Evie's eyes had darkened.

Hazel eyes, he noticed, which were just perfect framed by that dark blonde hair with its distinct auburn tint. Very expressive eyes, as well. He wanted to offer reassurance now. Comfort, even.

'It's a relatively common congenital heart defect,' he told her. 'And we have a few things we can do to treat it. She's going to stay here as well so I'm taking over her case. I'll do whatever I can to help her.'

'Like what?'

'We've started some medications. A prostaglandin

that can temporarily maintain the patency of the ductus arteriosus. Do you know what that is?'

Her nod was thoughtful. 'It's a little vessel that lets blood bypass the lungs until the baby is born, isn't it? And then it should close. That's often when congenital heart problems become obvious, isn't it?'

'Yes. Or they can become rapidly much worse, which is why we're going to try and keep it open. We can use inotropic agents to deal with heart failure symptoms as well. And tomorrow morning, after I've had some sleep, we're going to take Grace to the cath lab. I may be able to open the narrowed area of the aorta with a balloon. She's probably going to need surgery but I'd like to make sure she's completely stable before that happens.'

Evie nodded again. And then she smiled at him. 'Sounds like you know what you're doing, Mr Walker.'

Wow...that was some smile...

'Ryan, please...'

'I'm glad you were here.'

He could see something other than anxiety in her eyes now. Hope. Along with trust. He liked that. He'd better make sure he didn't do anything to make it vanish.

'Me, too...' He smiled back at her. 'It's not every job that starts with a roller-coaster like this. A glitzy party, an abandoned baby...a partner in her rescue.' He stood up and held out his hand. 'It was nice to meet you, Evie. Unforgettable, in fact.'

She hesitated for a moment but then put her hand in his. He squeezed it and gave it a gentle shake. Maybe he wanted to check whether that odd heat was still there when his hand touched hers.

And it was…

He let go instantly, the sea of red flags waving in his peripheral vision. 'I'd better get some sleep if I want to be on top of my game in the morning. The bedrooms are that way, yes?'

'Yes.' Evie was getting to her feet. 'I'd better get home as well. I'll see you tomorrow… Ryan.'

He watched her head towards the elevators. He was smiling again, he realised. Because of the extraordinary evening he'd had?

Or because he was going to see Evie Cooper again tomorrow?

Oh, man…he was overtired, that's what it was. He needed sleep and he needed it now.

'Hey, Evie…isn't that where you work?'

'Turn the television off, Bobby. And find your shoes. Stella's going to walk you to school this morning.' Evie walked past her youngest sibling on the way to put his lunch box into his schoolbag. And then she stopped as she heard a voice she recognised.

Theo Hawkwood. Standing outside, beneath the sign above the main entrance that named Hope Hospital.

'Yes,' he was saying. 'We're looking after this baby, who has been named Grace by our staff, but what we'd really like is to locate her mum. We're worried that she may be in need of medical attention herself.'

The camera shifted to focus on the man standing beside Theo and Evie caught her breath.

Ryan Walker…

He was looking directly into the camera. 'If you're listening,' he said, as if speaking directly to Grace's mother, 'please know that there are people who want to help. We understand that circumstances might seem impossible right now but please come and talk to us. You won't be in any trouble. We just want to make sure that you're okay.'

How could anyone resist that plea? And that smile…?

It had haunted Evie when she'd finally got to her bed last night and to have him here, practically in the living room of her house so early this morning, was quite a shock. He had scrubs on now and looked every inch the medical specialist that he was. Strange that shapeless clothes like that—the opposite end of the spectrum from the tailored tuxedo she'd first seen him wearing—could make someone look even more attractive.

Disturbing, that's what it was.

A policeman was talking now. 'Someone may have been helping with this birth, or have noticed something unusual happening. Anyone with any information can ring the confidential number on the screen now…'

Evie turned away from the news broadcast and went to the bottom of the stairs.

'Stella? Are you out of bed yet? You've got fifteen minutes. You're taking Bobby to school this morning, or have you forgotten?'

Her sister appeared at the top of the stairs. 'You don't need to shout,' she muttered. 'I'm onto it.'

'Where's Peter?'

'Asleep. He was still out at band practice when I got home from the disco last night.'

'Knock on his door. He'll be in trouble if he's late again.'

Ten-year-old Bobby tugged on Evie's sleeve. 'Have you seen my shoes?' Then he spotted his older sister. 'Hey, Stella… They found a baby in a cardboard box at Evie's hospital last night.'

'Really?'

'I found it, actually,' Evie told them. 'Her. We needed a name so I gave her Mum's name—Grace.'

'Wow…' Bobby's eyes were wide. 'Wait till I tell the kids at school. You'll be famous.'

'Don't think so.'

'Where did she come from?' Stella had reached the bottom of the stairs. 'Where's the mother?'

'We don't know. We think she's really young and was probably too scared to even tell anyone about the baby.'

'That's really sad,' Stella said. 'Hey… You like babies. Maybe you could look after her? The way you used to look after us when we were little.'

'I'm still looking after you.' Evie shook her head, suddenly wearied by more than not having had enough sleep last night. Was this how her family would always see her? As someone who existed only to look after others? It had been a no-brainer that she had stepped up to care for her much younger siblings after her mother had suddenly died but it seemed like it wasn't just her dreams for her career that she'd lost along with her mum—it was also a life where she was important for who she was herself and not simply what she could do for others.

'It's lucky I love you so much,' she added, with a

small sigh. 'Go and get some breakfast, Stella. And remind Dad to check his blood sugar. I've got to get going. I want to visit baby Grace before I start work, if I can.'

Susie was in the changing rooms when Evie went to deposit the scrubs she had worn home last night into the laundry bag.

'How's Grace?'

'Holding her own,' Susie responded. 'They're going to be ready for her up in the cath lab soon. Do you want to come and see her first?'

'I need to be on the desk pretty soon. I haven't got time to change.'

'Just put a gown on over your street clothes. And some booties over your shoes.' Susie was smiling. 'She's kind of your baby, Evie. You probably saved her life last night so I think you should go and visit.'

Evie didn't need any more encouragement. She slipped a disposable gown over her skirt and blouse and went into the NICU. Past Alfie's spot and on to an area that had far more equipment surrounding the incubator. The name tag on the end said simply 'Baby Grace' and there she was, naked, except for a tiny nappy, and lying on her tummy amongst a tangle of tubes and wires.

'Ohh...' Evie bent over the incubator, reaching out to touch the plastic walls that were keeping the temperature and oxygen level constant for the infant.

Janine walked past with another baby in her arms. She smiled at Evie.

'You can touch her,' she said. 'Through the porthole. Why don't you hold her hand and tell her that everything's going to be okay? She might remember your voice from last night.'

Evie cleaned her hands with gel from the nearby dispenser and then cautiously put one hand through the porthole. She touched the tiny starfish hand looking so pink against the pristine mattress and she had to blink away tears as she felt the miniature fingers respond and turn to curl around her forefinger. The way they had around Ryan's finger last night.

It felt like trust.

It felt like those tiny fingers were touching her heart, not her finger.

It felt like love...

Evie was so entranced she barely noticed the figure approaching Grace's incubator but she knew who it was well before he arrived. Like the signals the baby's touch was sending, she felt the way the air changed around her—as if it was full of static electricity.

'How's our baby this morning?' Ryan asked.

Evie had to smile. *Our* baby. But it didn't sound silly. They'd found Grace together and it gave them a bond. It felt like she already knew this man.

More than that. It felt like there was a real connection between them.

She could only meet his gaze briefly. It had been enough of a shock to see him on the television screen this morning. To be standing close enough to be aware of the heat of his body was almost overwhelming. If she touched his hand, the way she was still touching Grace's, she was quite sure she'd get that startling sensation as if her skin had suddenly woken up from a very deep hibernation.

She watched him from the corner of her eye as he checked the various monitors attached to the baby. Maybe he'd felt that skin tingle as well. Evie hadn't missed how quickly he'd pulled away from the handshake he'd offered at the end of the extraordinary evening they'd had yesterday. She hadn't been surprised, either. He would dismiss an unexpected attraction to someone like her, wouldn't he? For heaven's sake, he had a girlfriend who looked like a supermodel but was probably a brain surgeon or something.

People needed someone they could relate to, didn't they? The young doctor she'd fallen so hard for in her first hospital had dumped her when he'd attracted the interest of a clever colleague and she'd been a trainee nurse then. Now she was only a receptionist and she'd been reminded of that when Ryan had expected her to know what a coarctation of the aorta was. Thank goodness she'd remembered enough of an anatomy class to know what a ductus arteriosus was, so she hadn't looked like a complete idiot.

'I think we're good to go,' Ryan said. He glanced at Evie. 'Do you want to come and observe?'

The invitation was shocking. As if she was a real colleague. An equal.

'Ah…no, I can't. I've got work waiting.'

'No problem. I'll come and let you know how it went, if you like.'

'Please do.' She caught his gaze this time and it was suddenly too hard to look away.

Such blue eyes. There was a warmth there, as well. And confidence.

It was only then that Evie remembered that he'd

been alone by his car last night. Without the flashy girlfriend.

And he'd been waiting for *her*...

She also remembered her necklace at that instant but this was no time to ask where it might be now. Ryan was busy unhooking some of the monitors. An alarm beeped and Janine was there in an instant.

'Ready to go? I'll come with you.'

Evie watched them leave, rolling the incubator in front of them.

Ryan had invited her to go with them. To observe the procedure that Grace was about to undergo. That was even more astonishing than it would have been if he'd made it obvious that he was attracted to her.

Astonishing. And disturbing.

She didn't want him to think of her as an equal colleague. Or to find her attractive. Or for anything to happen between them other than what had already happened—the bond they had with that poor, abandoned baby.

She watched the doors slide shut behind him. It was time to take off her gown and booties and go and do the job she was paid for. There'd be extra work today after the gala last night. She needed to make sure the conference area had been left in perfect condition because there was an international gathering happening there in a few days' time, looking at innovations in caring for very low birth weight babies.

There was no sign of Ryan by the time she went through the unit doors herself but Evie found herself staring at the waiting area as if she could see him.

Oh, boy... She was kidding herself, wasn't she,

thinking that something happening between them was
the last thing she'd want?

It was hanging there in space.

Like a fantasy.

One that was almost close enough to touch, even.

CHAPTER FOUR

THEO HAWKWOOD WAS waiting for Ryan when he came out of the catheter laboratory later that morning.

'How did it go?'

'She's stable. I've just been reviewing all the films from the procedure and writing up my report. I'll send you a copy of that. I've widened the coarctation but we'll have to wait and see if it's enough.'

'Did you try and close the VSD?'

He shook his head. 'No. It's small enough not to be a problem and it may well start closing on its own. We'll keep an eye on her but it would take a concerning failure to thrive to be an indication for an invasive intervention like a closure device or surgery. Often, that's not done until much later in childhood, anyway.'

'Where is she now?'

'Back in NICU. I'm just on my way to see her. Do you want to come along?'

'No. I'll pop in later. I've got the police due in my office for an update soon and then back-to-back meetings this afternoon.'

'Was there any response to the television broadcast this morning?'

'A lot of calls, apparently, from people who thought they heard someone screaming or noticed bloodstains somewhere. Seems like there were a lot of people carrying boxes around the city last night, as well. They're following up potential leads but the mother hasn't made any contact.'

They walked towards the elevators together.

'How did you find the facilities in the catheter laboratory?' Theo asked. 'And the team?'

'Couldn't be happier,' Ryan told him. 'It's as good as you promised it would be.'

'And your apartment? I was very pleased when they told me they'd secured the penthouse of that new development that's so nearby. Hope it's not over the top but you did say you'd like something high-end.'

'I only saw it briefly,' Ryan told him. 'Long enough to dump my bags and get changed for the gala but it looks perfect. I stayed here last night in case I was needed.' He grinned. 'The staff bedrooms for Intensive Care are pretty high-end. Never had anything like that in Sydney, that's for sure. En suite bathrooms, even.'

'We want the best staff in the world here,' Theo said. 'And that means we need to look after them. I hope you're going to take this afternoon off to get properly settled in your apartment.'

'Yes. I need to dig something other than my tuxedo out of my bags. And sort out a car. I don't want to keep my rental too long and I need something a bit more solid than a sports car. I like to get away sometimes and do a bit of mountain walking.'

'Let me know if there's anything we can do to help you settle in.'

'Thanks. I might need some direction to local stuff. You don't know if there's a rugby club that might welcome a newcomer?'

'Ask Evie,' Theo told him. 'She's my go-to person for anything that needs doing or finding.' He pushed the button for the elevator. 'I must get my secretary to order some flowers for her. She was largely responsible for the success the gala was last night.' He sighed as they stepped through the doors. 'It was a shame she didn't get there to enjoy it herself.'

'Wasn't she working?'

Theo looked surprised. 'Not officially, but she does put in a lot of unofficial hours. If someone needs her, she's there.' He was smiling. 'She's one of a kind, our Evie.'

She certainly was.

Ryan was bemused to see her behind the reception desk as he headed into the PICU. Did she have a hand in every job that needed doing around here? She wasn't wearing scrubs or a gown now, just a plain shirt and a dark skirt that clung to her petite figure and made her look…delicate. Like a ballet dancer or something. So unlike any of the women he would normally be attracted to, but the pull was most definitely there. He paused by the desk.

'What are you doing out here?' he asked.

Evie's eyebrows rose. 'This is where I work,' she said. 'In Reception.'

'But I thought you were a nurse. You were in scrubs last night. And in the unit this morning.'

Her cheeks went very pink. 'I'm allowed to help out sometimes. With the babies.'

There was a story here. It wasn't so much the embarrassment that gave it away but the look in her eyes that made him think that something had happened to Evie. Something sad. Painful, even.

And he wanted to know what it was.

'Have you seen Grace since she got back?'

'Yes...' Evie's eyes brightened. 'She's looking better. Janine said I might be allowed to have a cuddle later.'

He held her gaze. He wanted to hear more about what seemed like a rather unusual receptionist's role.

Evie looked away. 'I almost became a paediatric nurse,' she said quietly. 'I had to give up my training because...because of family circumstances.'

'Ah...' Ryan put two and two together. She must have fallen pregnant during her training and decided to give up on her career. 'Yes, Janine mentioned your kids last night.'

'They're not *my* kids, exactly.' Evie opened her mouth to say something else but then shook her head. The phone on her desk began ringing at the same moment and she reached for it without hesitating.

'ICU, Evie Cooper speaking... Yes, of course, no problem... I'll find it for you right now...' She tucked the phone between her ear and her shoulder and began tapping on her computer keyboard. 'It's a long story,' she whispered to Ryan, excusing herself. 'Some other time...'

Ryan leaned over the counter. 'I'll hold you to that,' he murmured. 'I like stories...'

He gave himself a mental slap that coincided with the doors sliding open to let him into the unit.

What was he thinking? He'd been practically flirting with Evie Cooper just then and she *so* wasn't his type of woman.

It was obvious that everybody around here thought very highly of Evie as a responsible and helpful person. Maybe to outward appearances she was simply a receptionist but Ryan was quite sure there was more to Evie than a secretarial-type position.

Theo Hawkwood thought she was wonderful enough to send flowers to. Nobody had blinked when Evie had gone into the procedures room with the team in those first, tense minutes after finding the baby yesterday. She'd been wearing scrubs as if it was a completely normal thing for her to do. She'd been sitting beside Grace's incubator this morning, holding the baby's hand, for heaven's sake, giving the same impression of a deep involvement that he'd been aware of when she'd been waiting to find out how Grace was late last night.

No woman he'd ever seriously flirted with would bond with a baby like that. If they did, he would have been off like a shot. A hint of wanting something like that in their own future would have been just as offputting. Ryan Walker had no interest in getting caught up in anything that might be pointing towards marriage. Or a family. Or anything that was going to interfere with what mattered most in his life.

His job, first and foremost.

His lifestyle was just as important, but only because he'd learned to craft it to support his career. Both his love of sporting activities and the type of women with whom he chose to share his time—and his bed— were a means to stay healthy. To combat stress as much as to provide pleasure. To make sure his focus on his patients and the sometimes extreme challenge of the kind of surgery he was so good at was always the best it could be.

He was focusing now, as he reached baby Grace's incubator and picked up her chart to check all the recordings made since she'd left the catheter laboratory. Her heart rate and rhythm, arterial blood pressure, oxygen saturation levels, the doses of medication that had been administered and any response—there was a lot of clinical data to review.

'She's a darling, isn't she?' Janine appeared beside him, a soft blanket draped over her arm and a bottle of milk in her hand. 'Just the sweetest little thing...'

Ryan's response was no more than a huff of sound. Grace was a patient and he didn't get emotionally involved with patients. Or their families. If you did, it could interfere with making clinically sound judgements. It was best for everyone concerned if he kept his emotional distance and that was a skill he had honed just as effectively as his surgical prowess.

Better, perhaps, given that he'd been doing exactly that for pretty much his entire life.

'I'm a bit worried about her feeding,' Janine added. 'She's not taking to the bottle as well as I'd like.'

'Could be too tiring for her. It often happens with cardiac issues.'

'Hmm...' Janine opened the incubator and was rearranging the monitoring leads and IV lines to enable her to pick the baby up. 'If her temperature and oxygen saturation stays stable, we could put her in a crib rather than an incubator, do you think? It makes for easier access.'

'We'll review everything tomorrow. I'd like to do another echo, as well.'

Janine settled the wrapped baby in her arms and offered her the bottle but the baby whimpered and refused the teat.

'If she won't feed, we'll need to put in a nasogastric tube, as well.'

Janine sighed. 'I hope that won't be needed. She needs the human contact as much as anything. I might see if Evie's got time to stay for a bit after work today.'

'Evie?' Ryan blinked.

'She's our secret weapon.' Janine smiled. 'Our baby whisperer. She does cuddling shifts for us and I can assure you they make a difference. If anyone could persuade Grace here to accept a bottle, I reckon it would be our Evie.'

This was getting worse.

Evie Cooper was obviously some kind of angel when it came to sick babies. A born mother. The kind of woman who was patient and loving and loyal. The kind who would fall in love and probably stay that way for ever unless she had her heart broken.

The kind of woman that Ryan wouldn't go near romantically in a million years.

So what was with this odd pull he was feeling towards her?

It had to stop. Right now. It wasn't as if he had the excuse of extreme fatigue from jet lag any more. Or that he was caught up in a rather extraordinary event.

He had his first patient in his new job and this was the only thing he should be thinking about.

It was time to dismiss Evie Cooper from his thoughts.

'Things look stable,' he told Janine. 'Call me if you have any concerns. You've got my mobile number. I'm going to disappear for a while so I can find a change of clothes.'

'Oh, that's right…you stayed here last night, didn't you?'

'Yes. I might wear these scrubs home. I'd look a bit strange driving through Cambridge in a tuxedo at this time of day.' He turned back for a moment. 'Talking of tuxedos, is there a drycleaner's anywhere near here?'

'Yes, just a block or so away. Ask Evie for the address when you go past the desk. She knows everything.'

'Thanks.' But Ryan had no intention of stopping to ask Evie anything. He'd collect his clothes and then escape as quickly as possible. With any luck, she'd be absorbed by a phone conversation or, even better, away from her desk running some message and he wouldn't even see her.

He could find the drycleaner's himself.

Evie was doing her best to peel off feelings of guilt along with her street clothes as she changed into clean scrubs after her working day was complete.

This had to be the first time in eight years that she hadn't been home to put dinner on the table for two nights in a row but it was eight years, for goodness' sake. Surely she was allowed to start claiming a little more time just for herself?

Okay, Bobby was only ten years old but he was quite capable of feeding himself with some beans on toast, or something, and that wouldn't be necessary unless seventeen-year-old Peter had scoffed the leftovers of that enormous casserole she'd prepared in advance for last night when she'd known she'd be caught up with the gala. A not unlikely scenario, she sighed, pulling out her phone. Pete had had hollow legs ever since he'd become a teenager. She sent a text message to her father to check, and she was pulling disposable booties over her footwear when the response pinged in.

I've sent Bobby out for fish and chips. What time will you be home? Washing's piling up!

She sent a message back.

Turning phone off now. See you later.

Her family knew that she had to turn her phone off if she was going to spend any time in the ICU because they could interfere with things like IV infusion pumps.

They would just have to cope without her. What if she got run over by a bus or something? They'd have to cope then and she knew they were quite capable of doing so. They were all just too used to having her there. A substitute mother. The homemaker. It wasn't that she didn't love to spend time with her family and taking care of everybody had been such a huge part of her life for so long it wasn't going to stop anytime soon.

It was just that, right now, baby Grace was more important.

That Janine had specifically asked for her help to feed Grace was a request that Evie had no intention of refusing.

'It could take a while,' Janine told her, as she handed her the warm bottle of milk. 'If she gets breathless, she'll need a break. If she falls asleep, you might have to try and persuade her to wake up again. I'd really like to see her get a full feed on board. If her weight starts dropping, we'll have to give her a nasogastric tube.'

'She's got enough tubes and wires already.' Evie settled herself in the chair as Janine wrapped the baby and checked that none of the lines or wires had been displaced.

'My thoughts exactly.' Janine nodded. 'I'm heading off now, but any of the guys here will help if you have any worries. Thanks for trying this, Evie.'

Evie felt the weight of the baby snuggling into the crook of her arm. 'It's my pleasure.'

It was.

She looked down into the dark eyes staring up at her and felt her heart squeeze in a mix of protectiveness and pure love.

'Hello, wee Grace,' she whispered. 'Are you hungry, darling?' She stroked the tiny cheek with her finger and the baby turned towards her, her mouth opening. She eased the teat of the bottle into place. 'There you go.' She smiled. 'Mmm...'

Janine shook her head. 'How did you do that?'

'She was hungry, that's all.'

Both women watched the sucking movements of the baby.

'Not strong,' Janine murmured. 'But at least she's getting some nourishment.'

'I'll stay here till she's had a good feed,' Evie promised. 'Even if it takes all night.'

Each time Grace pulled back from the bottle, Evie held it up to see how much milk she had taken but the level was only dropping slowly, mil by mil. When the feed was almost halfway through, Grace fell asleep. Very carefully, Evie eased the small bundle upright, to hold her against her shoulder. She rubbed the tiny back and patted it, hoping that either Grace would burp or she would wake up and realise that she was still hungry. She was pretty sure that she had a window of two hours before a fresh batch of formula would need to be made and she still had plenty of time but it was always one of the nurses who prepared a baby's bottle and recorded amounts taken in a feed, so Evie looked around to see if she could catch the eye of a staff member who wasn't too busy so that she could ask for advice.

The eye she did catch was an unexpected one. What was Ryan Walker doing here at this time of the evening? He responded to her surprised gaze by coming towards her quiet corner of the unit.

'I heard they might be going to call you in,' he said. 'NICU's secret weapon.'

His smile made Ellie's toes curl.

'How's it going?'

'She managed half the bottle but she's sound asleep now. I'll wait for a while in case she wakes up and then I can try again. Did you come in to check up on her?'

'Yes and no. I've got my first theatre case tomorrow morning. An eight-week-old boy who'll be coming in to the NICU after surgery. I'm just getting all my ducks in a row.'

Evie nodded. 'What's the case?'

'An atrioventricular septal defect repair.' Ryan pulled up another chair and sat down beside her, as if having a chat was the real reason he was in the unit. 'It's complicated by involvement of the valves.'

'How do you fix it?'

His eyebrows rose. 'You really want to know?'

Evie nodded.

'Well, we use a patch made of synthetic material to repair the defect in the AV septum. And then I'll have to attach the deformed parts of the valves to the new septum to make sure they can function effectively.' His gaze was intense. 'You are really interested in this stuff, aren't you?'

Evie nodded again, but she couldn't hold that intense gaze. She dipped her head, which brought her lips into contact with Grace's head. Automatically, she pressed a soft kiss to the baby's hair. Grace stirred and then whimpered, so she moved her back into the crook of her arm and offered her the bottle again. At first she turned her head away, but the cheek stroking worked again and, a minute or two later, she was making another effort to suck. Evie was very aware that Ryan was watching the whole process.

'You've got the knack, all right,' he said. 'So, tell me. Why haven't you gone back to finish your nursing training? You're a natural.'

'I've never thought about it,' Evie admitted. 'When

I had to stop, it felt like the end of that dream. I guess life was so busy after that, it just slipped into ancient history. And I've probably forgotten more than I ever learned, by now.'

'So why did you stop?'

'My mum died.' Evie swallowed hard. Even after so long, the memory was painful. 'It was eight years ago now and it wasn't long before her fortieth birthday. It was a brain aneurysm.'

'That's a real tragedy…' She could sense that Ryan was still focused on her face. 'I get the impression that you were very close?'

'We were like sisters,' Evie said quietly. 'I know a lot of people say that, but it was true in our case. She had me when she was really young—only eighteen. She and Dad were together but they didn't get around to getting married until I was five. I got to be her brides-maid. And then they waited a long time before they had any more kids so it was just the three of us until I was nearly twelve and that was special. The three mus-keteers, Dad used to call us.'

'How many siblings have you got?'

'Three. Bobby, my youngest brother, was only two years old when Mum died. I was eighteen when he was born so I was already like a second mum for him. For them all, really.' Her smile was poignant. 'I guess I got an unexpected promotion.'

'So you gave up the career that you'd dreamed of?'

'It was the only thing I could do. And I wanted to do it—for Mum. Dad couldn't cope. He was shattered by losing Mum and then, a couple of years later, he got diagnosed with diabetes.'

Ryan exhaled in a sound of sympathy. 'You've certainly had your hands full.'

'I'm doing okay. The kids are great and I'm working again now. I just love this job.' Evie held up the bottle. 'Look at that, she's almost finished it.'

'Good work.'

'Could you help me put her back in the incubator? I'd hate to get these lines tangled.'

'Sure.'

Evie opened the cocoon of the blanket and Ryan reached in to take hold of the baby. There was no avoiding his hands touching her own. Brushing her breast, even, as he lifted the baby.

And it felt as if his hand was touching her bare skin. Evie cursed her propensity to blush and tried to cover it up by getting to her feet and folding the blanket. From the corner of her eye, she watched Ryan place the baby on the mattress and then turn away instantly to check the monitors.

She could still feel that touch. Even more than the first time it had happened, out in the car park, when—

'Oh…' Evie blinked. 'I meant to ask. Do you still have my necklace?'

Ryan stilled. 'It must be in the pocket of my tux,' he said. And then he frowned. 'I took it to the cleaners earlier today.'

'Oh, no… I hope it doesn't get lost. It was my mum's…'

She didn't need to tell him how special it was, she could see that he understood.

'I'll get in touch with them. Don't worry.'

'Okay, thanks.' Evie hesitated a moment but it was clear that Ryan was distracted.

'I'd better get going,' she said. 'I hear the laundry's piling up at home and nobody else seems to have figured out how to use that washing machine yet.'

Ryan simply nodded. 'Thanks for your help,' he said. 'See you tomorrow, maybe.'

Heart rate and rhythm. Blood pressure. Oxygen saturation...

Ryan focused on the monitors but he was aware of Evie walking away. Giving the almost empty bottle of milk to a nurse so that the baby's food intake could be recorded. Leaving the unit to go home to a family that had taken the place of the career she had wanted.

She would have made a damned good nurse, too.

And she was going home to tackle a pile of laundry?

Good grief... Did no one else help her with chores like that?

He was reading the figures on the monitors but there were other numbers in the back of his mind.

Evie's mother hadn't been quite forty when she'd died. She'd had Evie when she was eighteen. Eight years ago. That made Evie about twenty-eight or twenty-nine. She should be an independent young woman, enjoying the career of her choice. Or even starting her own family with the husband of her choice, maybe. And she would have had plenty of choice. Evie Cooper was stunning, both in her looks and her warm, generous personality. Did she even have a boyfriend? Just how much of her life had been put on hold for others?

Not that it was any of his business. And why did it matter so much? Ryan didn't get emotionally involved with the private lives of colleagues, any more than with his patients or their families, but that didn't mean he didn't care. That he couldn't encourage someone to get the most out of their lives.

Evie *was* a born nurse.

And, just because she was completely off limits as far as attraction might go, that didn't mean he couldn't be friends with her, did it? She hadn't thought about going back to finish her training but surely there was nothing that would be stopping her now—not if she was able to hold down a full-time job here at Hope Hospital.

He'd be willing to bet she hadn't forgotten everything she'd learned but it wasn't surprising that she might have lost some confidence along the way.

Maybe he could help. And maybe she could help him. He was new in town and she could help him get to know the place.

Yep...he could use a friend. Ryan pushed away any doubts that this might not be such a good idea. Like the memory of seeing her stroking the baby's cheek with that gentle touch. Or the way that brief body contact had made him feel when he'd lifted Grace from her arms.

He could control stuff like that, no problem.

And this could end up being a win-win situation for both of them.

CHAPTER FIVE

THEO HAWKWOOD WAS amongst the group of people at the ICU central station. Ryan Walker was also there and his friendly smile acknowledging Evie's approach made her realise how familiar it was becoming. In the space of a week or so, he had become a feature of her working life that was in danger of eclipsing everything else—with the exception of baby Grace, of course.

It didn't help that he was so friendly. He always seemed to find a moment to pause and chat with her when he went past her desk, or when she was sitting in the unit with Grace. For some reason, he had decided that she could help him with every query he had about the new city he was living in. She could have suggested he go online or purchase a tourist guide, but...if she was honest, she liked it that he wanted her opinions. That he seemed to value them. If he'd been flirting with her, she would have run a mile, despite the undeniable attraction, but he wasn't. He was just being friendly. Maybe all Australians were like that?

'Sorry to interrupt,' Evie said, 'but I have to get the new stationery order in by noon. I just wanted to check whether anything had been forgotten.'

'Pens,' Susie suggested. 'I always seem to be losing mine.'

'We're low on consent forms,' Janine added. 'And have you got ECG paper on that list? It didn't arrive last week, remember?'

'Let me check.' Evie lifted the clipboard in her hand. 'Yes, I've got a note of that. If you're really low, I could borrow some from the cardiology ward.'

She added a few more suggestions to her list and then caught Ryan's gaze. 'How's Grace doing?'

'That's why I'm here,' Theo put in. 'They're wanting to do another media update this afternoon. There's a reporter coming from a national newspaper as well.'

'She's holding her own,' Ryan said. 'But she's not gaining enough weight.' He raised an eyebrow. 'Maybe you should be in here more often for her feeds?'

'I'd love to,' Evie said, 'but I can only do it before and after work.' She tapped her clipboard. 'This is what I'm paid for, after all.' She knew she should be heading back to her desk, especially with Theo standing there, but she hesitated a moment longer, hoping to hear more about Grace's condition.

'That would make a great photo for the newspaper,' Susie suggested. 'Evie feeding Grace?'

'No *way*.' Evie was shocked. She needed to change the subject. Fast. 'Is there any news on finding Grace's mother?'

Theo shook his head. 'I think that's why the police want to make another public appeal. Maybe if we say something about the surgery she's going to need, it could make a difference.'

Evie's heart sank. 'So she is going to need surgery?'

'The coarctation seems to be narrowing again.' Ryan nodded. 'I'd like to see her put on a bit more weight before surgery but I don't think we can wait too much longer.'

Evie swallowed hard. 'It'll be dangerous, won't it? The surgery?'

'Open heart surgery on neonates always has risks,' Ryan said quietly. 'But we wouldn't do it if it wasn't necessary. And it's a procedure I've had experience with.'

Theo checked his watch. 'I have to go,' he said. 'HOD meeting. Would you believe that Christmas is on the agenda?'

'Oh, no…' Susie groaned. 'It's not even October.'

'Have you been in town recently?' Janine asked. 'Some of the shops are starting to put up decorations already. They'll be playing Christmas carols in no time.'

'This will be Hope Hospital's first Christmas,' Theo said. 'And it needs to be special. We're going to have to convene some committees to look at decorations. And the children's party, of course. We'll need a representative for Intensive Care. Anyone want to put their name forward for a committee?'

Everybody turned their heads at the same time and Evie's heart sank again. She didn't need her free time sucked up by new committee meetings. She wanted to spend every minute she could with baby Grace, especially if she had the trauma of heart surgery in the near future. Every minute would be precious in case… in case the worst happened?

No. There was a reason that Ryan Walker had been headhunted to take the job of operating on tiny little hearts. He was the best and she needed to have faith in him.

'Walk with me, Evie,' Theo said, coming out from behind the station. 'Let's talk about what committee you'd prefer. I reckon you need to be the chairperson this time, after your triumph with the gala.'

'What's going to happen, do you think?'

'Something spectacular.' Theo smiled. 'I'm thinking two super-sized Nordic trees to go outside the hospital and maybe another one for the main reception area. I imagine we'll have to get on with ordering them sooner rather than later.'

'No... I mean with baby Grace?'

'Oh...' Theo paused as they reached Evie's desk. 'I think she has a good chance of getting through this surgery. She'll be with us for a few weeks yet.' But he was frowning. 'Don't get too attached, will you, Evie? At some point, she'll have to be discharged. You know that, don't you?'

Evie nodded. Of course she did. 'But where will she be discharged to?'

'It's possible her mother will still come forward. Even if she's too young to care for her baby herself, she might have family who will want to adopt Grace.'

'But what if she doesn't?'

'Then she'll have to go into foster care until a family can be found for her. Try not to worry,' he added. 'There'll be someone special out there who will love her to bits, just like you do. I've been told there have been offers already, after the news first went public. Who knows? Baby Grace might have her own family by Christmas. Which reminds me...' Theo pulled out his phone. 'I need to ring home and check on Ivy. She isn't very well at the moment.'

'Oh, I'm sorry to hear that. I hope it's nothing serious.'

Theo shook his head. 'I don't think so. She just seems off colour. Not herself, you know?'

'I know.' Evie nodded. 'I used to worry about the kids all the time when they were young. They can get sick so fast and when they've just started school they pick up every bug that's going around. But they usually bounce back pretty fast, too.'

Theo smiled at her. 'You're right. I'm sure it's just a virus. Have a great day, Evie. I'll let you know about the Christmas committees later and you can choose.'

'Thanks, Theo.' Evie's tone was tinged with irony as she sat down behind her desk and brought the stationery order up on her computer screen. Another committee. How had that just happened so smoothly and now seemed to be something she had chosen herself?

'I've got an article you might like to read.'

'Oh...' Evie was heading into one of the private family rooms adjoining the reception area, later that afternoon, with fresh boxes of tissues in her arms. 'What kind of article?'

'It's a recent publication from one of the top medical journals. It'll tell you everything you might want to know about the surgery Grace is going to have.'

'From a medical journal?' Evie shook her head. 'It would be way over my head.'

'I doubt it.' But Ryan realised he might be taking the wrong route here to boost Evie's confidence and potentially persuade her to go back and finish her nursing training. He watched from the door as Evie swiftly tidied the room and replenished supplies. 'Sure, there might be some terminology you haven't come across yet but I could explain that.'

Evie took the photocopied pages from his hand as she came out of the family room. 'Okay…thanks.'

She only caught his gaze briefly but he could see the doubt in her eyes. There was something about the way the light was catching her face that made their colour unique. Golden brown. Tawny. Striking enough to make it hard to think of anything else for a moment. And she wasn't even wearing any make-up, as far as he could tell.

What you saw was what you got with Evie Cooper. She didn't wear make-up, she didn't do anything fancy with her hair and she wore clothes that looked like they came from a catalogue for office workers. And she was still beautiful…

Ryan cleared his throat. 'Fair's fair,' he murmured. 'You've been giving me a lot of great ideas. I went to that art gallery the other day. Kettle's Yard? It was amazing. And I checked out Parker's Piece, too, when I went for a run.'

'There'll be an ice skating rink there for Christmas. I think it opens about mid-November.'

'Fantastic. I love skating. I tried ice hockey for a while, back in high school.' Ryan was due to head into the paediatric intensive care unit to check that his latest young patient was ready to be transferred to the ward but he hesitated a moment longer. 'How 'bout you, Evie? Do you like skating?'

It was crazy, but he suddenly had an image of being on a rink with Evie. All bundled up with a woolly hat and gloves and a scarf, those gorgeous eyes sparkling in the cold. They were gliding around the rink, their arms linked. That wasn't beyond the boundaries of something that friends could do, was it?

'I'm useless at it,' Evie said. 'I used to take the kids a lot. Bobby still loves it but the others are too old now. They'd rather be hanging out with their mates. My oldest brother, Peter, plays guitar in a band with some friends from school.' She was behind her desk again now and looking like she wanted to get on with her work.

Ryan frowned. Evie often put herself down like that when all it took not to be 'useless' at something was a bit of practice. He could imagine her taking the children and then watching from the sidelines and it was a shame. She should be in the thick of things and having some fun.

'Where was that other place you said would be good for jogging?'

'I can't remember. Wandlebury Nature Reserve? A couple of miles out of town?'

'No. It was more central. My apartment's not far from here and I like to be able to head straight out from home. I don't get that much free time.'

'The Backs? That must be really close for you and it's gorgeous. Big stretch of reclaimed land that goes along the River Cam, behind the colleges. That's where I take Bobby when he wants to ride his bike.'

'That was it. Thanks.' Ryan headed into the PICU,

making a mental note to check out The Backs the next time he needed to run off any tension or fatigue.

'Okay, that's it.' Evie marched into the living room. 'I'm turning the telly off.'

'That's not fair.' Bobby scowled. 'I've done my homework.'

'It's a lovely sunny day. How often do we get that in a weekend? Haven't you got some friends you could go and play football with?'

Bobby shook his head. His father's head appeared above the newspaper he was reading.

'Evie's right, son. You should go and get a bit of fresh air and exercise.'

'I'm walking to the shops. I forgot to get mint sauce at the supermarket last night and we've got roast lamb for dinner. Who wants to come with me?'

Stella was sitting at the table, painting her nails. 'Not me. I'm meeting Lydia at the shopping centre later.'

'Make sure you're back in time for dinner.'

'Yeah, yeah… Who made you the boss?'

'That's enough, Stella,' her father growled. 'Get your shoes on, Bobby, and go with your sister.'

Bobby sighed heavily. 'Can I take my bike?'

'That's a great idea,' Evie said. 'We'll go along The Backs.' As she found their coats and a scarf for herself, she found herself wondering if Ryan had discovered the delights of those pathways yet. She hadn't seen so much of him in the last few days since he'd given her that article on the type of surgery that Grace was going to have. Had she been subconsciously avoiding him, perhaps? How embarrassing would it be if he asked her a simple question about that article and she had no idea what he was talking about?

At least she had the weekend to try reading it now. It would make a change from catching up on all the housework and laundry. This was only the second weekend since Grace had become a part of her life but two days away from the hospital and her new feeding duties felt far too long. Maybe she could escape for a few hours tomorrow and go in for a cuddling shift, at least.

A sunny autumn Saturday afternoon had brought lots of people to The Backs. Whole families out together. People jogging or walking dogs. Couples walking hand in hand. Even tourists taking in the views of the lovely old buildings as they experienced the classic punting on the River Cam. By the time they were on their way back from the shopping centre, Bobby was clearly enjoying his bike ride.

'Watch me do a wheelie,' he told Evie.

'Not on the path,' she warned him. 'And stay away from that pushchair.'

But Bobby was already speeding up, lifting the front wheel of his bike and pedalling even faster to keep his balance. Evie was being left well behind and watched with mounting concern as someone hauled their dog off the path to get out of Bobby's way. She heard them shout a rebuke and maybe that was what made Bobby lose his concentration. She could see the way the wheel in the air started wobbling and then seemed to turn sharply, pulling the bike off balance and sending Bobby crashing to the ground.

Oh, help...at least she'd nagged him into wearing

his helmet. Evie wasn't the only person running to see if he was all right. A jogger had zoomed past her and reached him first.

'You okay, buddy?'

She knew that voice. That accent. Not that she'd recognised Ryan's back as he'd gone past but why would she, when she'd never seen him dressed like this? In just a pair of shorts and a T-shirt. So much tanned skin on display was very disconcerting.

'Ryan...'

'Evie?' He spared her only a surprised glance before his attention was back on Bobby, who was still underneath his bike and clearly trying hard not to cry. He lifted the bike clear and Evie stepped closer to take hold of it. 'Anything hurting, mate?'

Bobby shook his head. But when he tried to move, his face twisted in pain and he cradled one arm against his chest as he rubbed it.

'Is your arm sore?' Ryan asked. 'Let's have a look.'

Bobby shrank back, turning towards Evie. 'I want to go home,' he said.

'It's okay, Bobby. This is Ryan. He's a doctor...a friend of mine from work.' She crouched down beside him, looking up to catch Ryan's gaze. 'This is Bobby, my little brother.'

'G'day, Bobby.' Ryan's smile and easy manner had probably endeared him instantly to any patients who were old enough to be wary of doctors.

Bobby stared at him as if he'd jogged in from another planet.

'Ryan's Australian,' Evie said.

'I know that.' Bobby seemed to have forgotten about

his sore arm. 'I've seen the crocodile hunter on television. He sounds just like him.'

'I haven't hunted any crocs lately,' Ryan told him. 'But I used to see lots of kangaroos on the golf course near to where I used to live.'

'Really?' Bobby's eyes were wide. 'Why were they on the golf course?'

'Nice big green space, I guess. Like this but without the river. Now...how 'bout that arm of yours? Can you wiggle your fingers?'

'Yeah... I think so...' Bobby held out his arm and demonstrated.

'Okay...tell me if this hurts.' Ryan gently examined his arm from the shoulder right down to his fingertips and Evie was relieved to see that Bobby could bend his elbow and wrist without it being painful.

'I don't think anything's broken,' Ryan declared. 'But there's probably a few bruises and he might have sprained that wrist. Keep an eye on it, and if it gets more painful or swells up, take him in for an X-ray.'

'Thanks.' Evie nodded. She was holding the bike with one hand, so she could gather Bobby under her other arm as he scrambled to his feet. She squeezed his shoulders. 'Next time, wheelies on the grass,' she scolded. 'You nearly ran over that poor dog.'

'That man shouted at me,' Bobby said. 'It made me lose my balance. But did you see before that? I smashed it.'

Ryan was grinning. 'I saw it,' he told him. 'And you did smash it. But practising on the grass, away from other people, isn't a bad idea, mate. And that way you won't risk smashing yourself or anyone else.' He was bouncing on his feet now and checking his watch. 'I'd better get going,' he said.

'Sorry,' Evie apologised. 'You must be freezing by now.'

'I'm fine. I just want to drop back to work and do a ward round before it gets dark. Hey...thanks for telling me about this place. It's awesome.'

'You're welcome. Give Grace a cuddle from me when you're in the NICU.'

An odd expression crossed Ryan's features that made Evie feel as if she'd overstepped some boundary. Embarrassed, she turned her head.

'You'll have to come back here in spring,' she said. 'It's a sea of daffodils.'

'What's that building over there?'

'All the buildings are part of the University of Cambridge. It dates back to 1209. Go and look at the grounds sometime.'

'Looks like part of a golf course from here.'

Bobby had fully recovered from the fright of his fall now. He took the handlebars of his bike from Evie's grip and offered Ryan a shy grin. 'Don't think there's any kangaroos.'

'No? Shame...' Ryan grinned back but then turned away, raising a hand in farewell. 'See you guys later.'

Bobby walked beside Evie instead of getting back on his bike. 'He's really nice, isn't he?'

'Yeah...' Evie watched the figure disappearing into the distance along the path. She could feel the distance increasing, as if something attached to herself was becoming tighter and tighter. She braced herself for the discomfort of it snapping. 'He really is...'

* * *

'Give Grace a cuddle from me...'

Evie's voice seemed to echo in the back of Ryan's head every time he was near the baby. Like now, as he held his stethoscope against that tiny chest to listen to her heart.

He had never 'cuddled' one of his patients.

He never would.

How unprofessional would that be?

It wasn't that he didn't care about them. He couldn't care more about their clinical outcomes. He found enormous satisfaction—joy, even, in a successful outcome and he had been completely gutted more than once when he'd lost a patient despite his best efforts.

But those emotions were about the case, not the person.

And, somehow, that careless remark of Evie's had planted the idea that maybe there was something wrong with him. What if he hadn't been in control for so many years and deliberately choosing to keep his distance from people to avoid the kind of pain that emotions automatically created? What if he wasn't even capable of feeling strongly about someone else?

Would that make him some kind of heartless monster?

The complete opposite of someone like Evie?

The abnormal heart sounds he could hear were getting louder again and Ryan suspected that the blood flow to the baby's lower body wasn't as good as it had been straight after the procedure to widen the narrowed part of the aorta. Grace started crying as he pressed the skin on her big toe to leave a pale spot, looking for evidence of how quickly the blood returned to make it pink again.

Something needed to be done. More tests, for starters. Consultation with the specialist paediatric cardiologists here at Hope Hospital. It would also be a good idea to start planning the intricate surgery that would be needed to try and correct the problems.

Ryan made notes on Grace's chart as her cries got louder and then hung it back on the end of her crib. He looked around to see if someone was also hearing the sound of a baby that needed attention. Feeding, maybe. Or a nappy change.

Or just a cuddle…

Yes… Janine was heading in his direction. He nodded at her as she leaned into the crib to pick up the baby.

'I'm going to ask one of the cardiology team to come in later today. We need a thorough review of Grace's progress.'

'At least she's put on a bit of weight. Thanks to Evie. I might see how quiet it is in Reception at the moment. She's still the only person who can persuade this little button to drink a whole bottle.'

And there she was again. In the back of his mind, as he headed to his office to make some phone calls to schedule tests and speak with his colleagues, even though he hadn't actually spoken to Evie since that chance encounter by the river.

He'd been shocked, to be honest, meeting her like that on his run the other day. She had told him that her youngest sibling had only been two years old when her mother had died, and that she'd stepped into the role of mothering him, but it was one thing to hear it and quite another to see it. To *feel* it.

The way that lad had looked to her for comfort when he'd been frightened by his fall. The way she had automatically gathered him close when he'd got to his feet. That bond was unbreakable. Ryan had the impression that Evie was the sun that her planet family revolved around and yet she still had more love to give.

To any and every baby that needed cuddling around here and most especially to the particular baby he'd just been to visit. He had a connection there that had nothing to do with the clinical case that baby Grace presented. He'd been there, with Evie, when they'd found the abandoned baby. He shared her interest in the ongoing investigation to try and find the baby's mother. He appreciated the amount of time and effort Evie was giving to Grace's care.

But he didn't share that emotional bond. He didn't feel it. There was a solid, if invisible wall there. A detachment that was welcome when it came to making decisions that could make the difference between life and death but, for the first time, Ryan had a niggle of doubt about whether it was a character strength or some kind of flaw.

It wasn't that he was an unkind person, he reminded himself later, when he had finished organising the next steps in Grace's care. He knew he was a good friend to people. A great lover, if the women in his life so far had been honest. He'd never had trouble winning the confidence and trust of his young patients or their families. His flaw, if that's what it was, was well hidden. So well hidden he hadn't actually given it any thought until now.

Until Evie had casually suggested that he could give Grace a cuddle on her behalf.

Shoving some paperwork to one side of his desk, he knocked something to the floor. Ryan bent to retrieve it.

Ah...the tickets to the charity ball next week. It was going to be a glamorous evening by the sound of things. Black tie. In one of Cambridge's top hotels. He'd better remember to go and collect his tuxedo from the drycleaner's. It had been ready for some time now, but he'd only taken note of the missed phone call and then forgotten about it.

The way he'd forgotten about that necklace that had been in the pocket of the jacket.

Oh, no... Ryan closed his eyes for a long moment. This time it was entirely his own fault that Evie was back on his mind. He felt guilty. More so, because she hadn't reminded him about it. Maybe he wasn't quite the kind and thoughtful person he had believed himself to be.

He opened his eyes. How could he make it up to her? The answer seemed to be staring him in the face in the form of those tickets.

Evie was always in the background, wasn't she? Doing things for others. Caring for her family. Caring for Grace. She'd been horrified at the idea of having her photograph taken for a newspaper article. According to Theo, she'd put in an enormous amount of work for the opening gala that first night he'd been here but she hadn't even attended the event herself. How was she going to find the person who would make her feel as special as she deserved to feel if she kept hiding herself away like that?

Evie Cooper deserved to find that person. She deserved to feel special for once, come to that. Like a princess instead of a Cinderella.

Oh, yeah…the more Ryan thought about it, the better the idea became.

Evie *would* get to go to the ball…and he was the one who could wave the magic wand.

CHAPTER SIX

'YOU'RE ASKING *ME* to go to a ball with you?'

Evie had never been this shocked in her life. The fantasy that Ryan Walker represented had suddenly sprung into life again. Okay, that wasn't entirely true. It had haunted her sleep, not to mention a few waking moments, ever since she'd first seen him, if she was honest with herself. Gathered momentum, even, after that meeting by the river. But she'd given herself a stern talking to and had it under control again.

Until now. He was asking her out on a date? Not just any kind of date but…a *ball*…?

'I just happen to have a spare ticket.' Ryan leaned further over the desk and gave her that smile that went straight to her toes. 'And I thought…who do I know that really, really deserves a great night out?'

Oh…something bigger than disappointment made Evie sink into her chair like a deflating balloon. It wasn't a date. He just wanted to offer someone his spare ticket.

A gift. Like charity…

'No…' Evie tried to look busy, rearranging some

items on her desk. 'Not my sort of thing. I wouldn't know anybody.'

'You'd know me.' Clearly Ryan wasn't going to give up. 'And you might meet someone new. Someone special, even...' His eyebrows were raised and, in combination with that lingering smile, the charm was being turned on full force.

'I don't want to meet someone special.' Her tone came out a lot more sharply than Evie had intended. No wonder Ryan looked taken aback.

'Why not?'

'Been there, done that.'

'And you've just given up?' Ryan blew out a breath. 'Man, he must have done a bit of a number on you.'

Evie shrugged. 'Haven't had time to think about it, really. I've got enough on my plate.'

'Exactly.' Ryan tapped the tickets on the top of the counter. 'That's why you need a night out with a mate. A bit of fun.'

But Evie shook her head. 'They take photographs at that kind of thing. Like *Chat Zone* did at our gala. Someone might think you were on a date. How embarrassing would it be if everyone knew you were there with...with a receptionist?'

Ryan's tone was astonished. 'Why on earth would that matter?'

'It just does.' Evie couldn't look at him. She wished he would go and get on with something important. Like checking on Grace.

But he leaned even closer. And lowered his voice. 'Tell me, Evie...what was it that your last boyfriend did for a crust?'

'He was a doctor. Training to be a surgeon.'

'Training to be a jerk, more like.' Ryan sounded so outraged on her behalf that Evie actually laughed. And immediately felt better. She could handle this.

'Why don't you ask Susie? Or Janine? I'm sure they'd love to go.'

'I think Susie's husband might object. And why would I want to talk shop when I'm out, anyway? Come on, Evie…' There was a plea in Ryan's voice. 'We're friends, aren't we?'

'Yes…'

'And friends help each other out. I need a plus one. I think you could use a night out. That's it. No agenda, no strings. There'll be some nice food and music and maybe some dancing. Do you like dancing?'

Oh…how long had it been since she'd been on a dance floor? It felt like a whole lifetime ago.

It wasn't a real date so she didn't have to angst about it being something so far out of her league or turning into anything that could cause heartbreak. It was, however, a chance to play a little with that fantasy and, heaven help her, that was appealing. Irresistible, even…

Her breath came out in a long sigh. 'If I say yes, will you go away and let me get on with my work?'

Ryan's smile widened into a grin. 'Absolutely.'

'Fine. Yes. I'll go with you. Leave the ticket with me and I'll meet you there, shall I?'

Ryan shook his head. 'It's not far from here. If the weather's okay, we could meet in the car park and walk and that will save any parking hassles.' He was still smiling. 'That's where we first met, remember?'

'Hmm…' Evie shook her head. 'Go away, Ryan. I'm busy.'

Except she wasn't that busy. Between administrative duties, greeting new visitors that arrived and looking after a mother who needed a break from the scary environment of the ICU that her baby had just been admitted to, there was too much time to start worrying about Friday night. It was a serious concern by the time she sat with Grace after work to feed her.

It was a *ball*. Far more glamorous than Hope Hospital's gala night had been and her best dress—that she hadn't got around to wearing anyway—had been barely adequate for such an occasion.

What on earth was she going to wear to this glitzy event?

The worry had turned into full-blown panic by the time she got home that evening.

'I won't go,' she finally decided, aloud to make it even more definite. 'Ryan will just have to find someone else.'

'Won't go where?' Stella demanded, coming up behind Evie as she was serving up the family's dinner. 'And who's Ryan?'

'It's nothing,' Evie muttered.

But Stella thought otherwise. 'Evie's got a boyfriend,' she announced at the table. 'And his name's Ryan.'

'Good for you,' her father said. 'Pass the potatoes, would you?'

'He's not my boyfriend,' Evie said. 'He's—'

'Nice,' Bobby put in. 'He helped me when I fell off my bike.'

'He's just a friend,' Evie said. 'And he has a spare ticket for a ball on Friday. But I'm not going because I haven't got anything to wear.'

'You should go,' her father said. 'You deserve a night out.'

'But—'

'Your mother used to love a dance,' he added. 'You should have a look at that box of old dresses of hers up in the loft.'

Stella grinned. 'Cool. I want to see, too.'

The dishes were left undone for some time after dinner that evening. Even Bobby and Peter hung around to see what came out of the box.

'This one,' Stella decided.

'But…it's brown…' Evie stared at the dress. 'How old-fashioned is that?'

'It's vintage,' Stella told her sister. 'It's on trend. And…look at the label. It's French.'

Evie held the dress against her body. The built-in, silky slip was black, but the actual dress was a chocolate-brown lace. It had a scooped neck and a dropped waistline that gave it a Roaring Twenties look. Certainly different… She didn't remember her mother wearing it, but she did remember how much she had loved to go out dancing in the days before the younger children had come along. She remembered how beautiful she'd seemed—like a princess to that young Evie—and how confident she'd been as she'd headed out to do something she loved.

Maybe Evie needed to channel a side of her mum that she'd almost buried under the endless tide of childcare and household duties over the years.

'You know what?' Stella was actually looking excited. 'I've been watching videos about how to do these amazing plaits. I could do your hair for you on Friday night. Let you use a bit of my make-up, even.'

How astonishing was this? Her family were looking at her as if she was...a *real* person? Someone who might have a life of her own? A boyfriend, even? Evie sucked in a deep breath. This could be it. Never mind any fantasies about Ryan Walker. This could be a chance to take a step into what could become a very different life.

'Thanks, Stella.' Her voice had a bit of wobble to it. 'I'd really appreciate that.'

Wow...

Ryan had guessed that Evie was hiding something special under her no-nonsense appearance but he could never have imagined it was anything quite this spectacular.

'You look...stunning...'

'Thanks.' Evie ducked her head with an appealing shyness. 'It's just an old dress that belonged to my mum.'

'It's not just the dress. Your hair...' Ryan couldn't stop staring. Intriguing braids were woven sideways around Evie's head, pulling the rest of her hair into soft loops at the base of her neck, and there were small, sparkly flowers dotted here and there.

'It's lucky I have a teenaged sister who's into watching "how to" videos on hair and make-up. It's a whole new world out there with online tutorials on anything at all.'

'Mmm.' Ryan wasn't going to comment on how different Evie looked wearing make-up but, oh, man... her eyes looked twice as big. She looked older than usual but, weirdly, more vulnerable at the same time. He was going to have to keep an eye on the men who would no doubt flock towards her tonight.

And they did.

Evie seemed disconcerted by the amount of attention she received and was apparently happy to stay close to the only person she knew in this crowd. It was Ryan who found her a glass of champagne, kept the conversations going with each new group of people who wanted to talk to them, and led her onto the dance floor the moment he saw another man approaching with the clear intent of asking her.

Who knew that Evie would be able to dance this well? One dance led to another. And another. Evie's cheeks were pink and her eyes shining but she was loving it and he could feel her confidence growing. She was *glowing*...

She was full of surprises tonight, that was for sure, but the thing that took Ryan totally by surprise was the way it was making *him* feel.

Blown away. Protective. Possessive, even, which was stupid because one of the reasons he'd thought this was a good idea was the idea that Evie *could* meet someone new. The kind of man who would realise how lucky he was to find someone with such a warm heart and total devotion to her family.

Maybe it was enough that she was gaining confidence. In which case, he could simply relax and enjoy her company. It was only one night, wasn't it? It wasn't as if it was going to lead to anything more. Ryan only had to remember how close Evie was to her family to know beyond a shadow of doubt that she would never fit into his life but he was very practised at enjoying something temporary, even if it was holding such a beautiful woman in his arms only to dance with her.

Close to midnight, Evie declared that it was time she went home.

'I'm not used to this.' She laughed. 'I might turn into a pumpkin. You stay if you want to, Ryan. It's not that far to walk to my car.'

'Don't be daft.' Ryan headed to the cloakroom with her. 'I'm not about to let you walk the streets alone. I've had enough, anyway.'

'It was wonderful, though, wasn't it?' Evie's face was still glowing as she wrapped herself into her warm coat.

'It was.' Ryan's smile felt different. Almost poignant. He was too used to occasions like this. Jaded, even? He had experienced it through someone else's eyes tonight, however. Someone who had stopped hiding in the background and come out of their shell. Come to life in a way that had made this evening unique. Magic, in fact.

They walked back towards Hope Hospital.

'I can't believe I've been out dancing in one of Mum's dresses,' Evie told him quietly. 'It's really special. She loved to dance. She was really good at it.'

'So are you.'

'Not like she was. She was amazing at everything, especially being a mum. I've tried so hard to be like her but…we all still miss her so much. Apart from Bobby, maybe. He was too young to really remember her.'

Ryan was silent for a long minute. He could imagine how heartbreaking it had been for Evie to lose her mother and he was sad for the young Evie who had tried so hard to step into her mother's shoes and be everything for her family, sacrificing her own needs along the way.

As they entered the main gates of the hospital and headed for the staff car park, his steps slowed.

'You've done an amazing thing for your family, Evie,' he said. 'For a very long time. They can cope with less of you now, you know. Maybe it's time to chase your own dreams again.'

Evie stopped walking but said nothing.

'You could do anything you want to do,' Ryan said softly, holding her gaze. 'Be anything that you want to be.'

She broke the eye contact but still said nothing. She turned her head, as if searching for something, and, a moment later, she caught her bottom lip between her teeth.

'I can never see those rubbish bins without thinking about Grace,' she murmured. 'About the way we found her.'

About the way they'd met…

As Evie turned back, Ryan had the curious sensation that he was falling into those extraordinary eyes of hers. They shone with something that looked like hope. For baby Grace's future, he wondered, or for her own?

He couldn't look away and, apparently, neither could Evie.

And then it happened. Ryan wasn't quite sure who

moved first. Or why neither of them realised that this probably wasn't a good idea but the instant of time when it could have been avoided was gone so fast it hadn't really existed. He leaned down. Evie came up on tiptoes and he was kissing her.

She was kissing him back. There was no mistaking that response and that first touch and taste of her mouth drove any doubts about the wisdom of doing this far, far away from Ryan's consciousness. Something more powerful than anything he'd ever experienced before had been unleashed.

He broke the kiss, only to start another one. To draw her close to his body so that he could feel the shape of that slim body and inhale the delicious scent of her.

His voice was hoarse when he finally found it.

'Come home with me,' he whispered. 'It's just around the corner...'

It had been a fantasy come to life right from the start of this evening.

From the effort that Stella had put in to make her feel more beautiful than she ever had and the poignant moment when she had slipped into her mother's dress.

The glittering lights of the chandeliers in the hotel ballroom. The fizz of champagne on her tongue. The way every man in the room seemed to be looking at her and letting her know that she was, in fact, beautiful.

Dancing with Ryan...

And, as if that Cinderella experience hadn't been enough of a memory to treasure for ever, he'd kissed her.

Or maybe she had kissed him.

It didn't seem to matter. The fantasy wasn't over and she'd just been invited to step into it to a whole new level. To let herself believe, just for a little longer, that she *could* fall in love with someone like Ryan Walker.

That he would love her back...

She should have said no, of course, but that would have broken the spell instantly and Evie just couldn't do it.

She didn't want to. And hadn't Ryan just told her that she could do anything she wanted? That she could be anything she wanted to be?

At this moment, the only thing she wanted to be was this man's lover.

And here she was, in an apartment that was luxurious enough to be simply the background of a continuing fantasy but it was real. She could feel the soft carpet beneath her feet when she kicked off her shoes. Could feel the touch of Ryan's hands as he helped her out of her coat and then reached for the zipper at the back of her dress. He was kissing her again as the silk and lace puddled at her feet and now the reality was the touch and taste of his lips and his tongue, the shaft of desire—strong enough to be painful—as his hands gently cupped her breasts. The strength in his arms as he effortlessly scooped her up and carried her to his bed.

It was a dream. An unexpected, exquisite dream.

But Ryan had said that, as well, hadn't he? That it was time for her to chase her own dreams?

Evie could do that. At least for this utterly magic night.

Tomorrow was another day.

CHAPTER SEVEN

IT WAS WELL before dawn when Evie arrived at Hope Hospital the next morning.

She should be exhausted, she realised, because it was only a few hours since she'd tiptoed back into her own house, being very careful not to wake any of her family, and she hadn't slept a wink during the time she'd spent in her own bed.

But she had never felt more...alive than she did right now. So alert that every sense seemed heightened. She was so aware of the chill of the morning air as she pulled it into her lungs and she caught the delicious smell of hot coffee from somebody's takeaway mug as they came out of the small café adjacent to the main reception area. The sound of a child's laughter floated through the doors of one of the wards she walked past on her way to the ICU and it made her smile.

Made her realise that this floating sensation was pure happiness of her own. The kind of happiness that came from having spent the most memorable hours ever in the arms of a man she realised she was hopelessly in love with.

The fantasy had refused to be put back into its box.

It had stayed with Evie as she'd lain in her own bed, staring at the ceiling, reliving every passionate moment of being with Ryan Walker. Holding onto the confidence he had inspired. The belief that, from now on, this was going to be *her* time. That her dreams could really come true.

She went straight to the changing rooms and pulled on a set of scrubs. Evie was as happy as she had ever been in her life but the fact that she had extra time to spend with Grace this morning added a new layer that made things seem just too good to be true. Taking the tiny baby into her arms and pressing the softest kiss to Grace's head was enough to bring tears to her eyes.

'You okay?' Janine had Grace's bottle in her hands.

'I'm great.' Evie blinked hard as she smiled up at Janine. 'Just...really happy. I love this wee girl...'

'We all do.' But Janine was frowning as she handed over the bottle. 'Keep an eye on her. She didn't have the best night and her last feed didn't go so well. Let us know if you need some help.'

Evie nodded but her confidence was as heightened as her senses were. She was the baby whisperer, wasn't she? Intensive Care's secret weapon. She could do this. She could do anything she wanted to do. Ryan had been totally sincere when he'd told her that.

Ryan... Evie stroked Grace's cheek and offered her the bottle. Would he come to check on Grace before he started his theatre list this morning? While she was still in here, perhaps? What would happen in that moment when her gaze caught his? A private communication that would let her know that the sex had been as amazing for him as it had been for her?

A promise, perhaps, that it was going to happen again?

The anticipation of that look was enough to steal her breath away. Maybe baby Grace picked up on something being very different with Evie this morning because she made only a half-hearted attempt to suck and then gave up, pulling her head back and starting to cry. Evie put the bottle down and rocked the baby, trying to soothe her.

'It's okay, sweetheart…everything's going to be okay… Have a little rest and then we'll try again…'

Cries became whimpers and then snuffles as Grace relaxed into sleep in her arms. Evie was watching her tiny face the whole time, her own head bent so close she could feel the baby's breath. She felt the exact moment when sleep made the little body go limp. She also felt the exact moment when Ryan arrived in the unit. She didn't look up, though. She wanted to savour this anticipation. To wait until he was right beside her before she caught his gaze because it was a moment that she wanted to be as private as it possibly could be.

When she did look up, it was even more than she could have hoped for. There was an expression on Ryan's face that looked as if he couldn't quite believe what he was seeing. A softness in his eyes that was an invitation to love…and be loved.

Without thinking, Evie lifted the small bundle she was holding towards him.

'Have a cuddle,' she said with a smile. 'It's the best thing, ever…'

The reaction to her suggestion was totally not what she had expected. Ryan seemed to rear back and the

expression on his face turned into something like...
disgust?

'She's not a toy,' he snapped. 'She's a patient. If
you're not feeding her, Evie, perhaps you can put her
back into her bed.'

Evie flinched at his tone and the movement was
enough to wake Grace. Frighten her, even, judging by
the way she arched her back and opened her mouth to
start crying again. Except no sound emerged and Evie
could feel the tension of the baby's body as she strug-
gled for more air.

It felt like Ryan wrenched the baby from her arms.

'Find Janine,' he ordered. 'And Susie, if she's
around.'

He put the baby into her crib, pulling the blanket
from around her. As Evie fled, she saw him unhooking
the stethoscope from around his neck and she could
hear one of the alarms on a monitor begin a strident
beeping.

The bristles of the scrubbing brush were rigid enough
to be painful if you pressed too hard but the stream of
warm water soothed any lingering discomfort.

It was just a shame that Ryan couldn't wash away
the internal discomfort that easily.

He'd hurt Evie. He'd never had any intention of
snapping at her like that but he'd been struggling already, totally floored by his first sight of Evie after that
astonishing night last night. Seeing her sitting there,
with her head bent over the baby, holding her as if she
was the most precious thing on earth.

For a moment, as he'd walked towards them, Ryan

had been sideswiped by a longing he'd never, ever expected to feel.

The longing for his own family...

And then Evie had looked up at him and her gaze was offering him all the love he could possibly want and she'd held the baby up to him, as if...as if it was their own child.

The shockwave had wiped out any errant longing. It had been like a slap in the face to remind him of exactly why he'd never allowed himself to feel anything like that and it had been replaced by a wash of anger that he had already gone too far down that path. It wasn't enough of a reason to excuse the way he'd snapped at Evie but the fact that the baby's condition had been clearly deteriorating at the same time simply confirmed every reason not to get emotionally involved. With anyone.

Stabilising the baby and running tests to find out what was going on had taken up the rest of the morning and now Ryan's afternoon elective theatre list had been pushed back and he was about to operate on baby Grace. He needed every ounce of focus to be on the job he had to do.

Gowned and masked, he stepped into Theatre. His patient was already waiting for him, unconscious and draped. It was easy to focus now. This wasn't a baby that had been cradled by the woman he'd made love to so recently. It was a tiny chest that needed to be opened with a scalpel.

A major blood vessel that had to be delicately separated from the tissue around it and then clamped on both sides of the deformed section that needed to be excised. Tiny stitches had to be placed with a precision that would ensure a completely stable join in the artery and, even though he would be able to relax into the painstaking task of closing the chest, Ryan wouldn't be thinking of anything else for some considerable time. Or *anyone* else. Grace's life might depend on that. His own well-being certainly did, too.

He stayed with his patient in Recovery until he thought it was safe to transfer her back to the NICU and then it took time to make sure the team was aware of everything that needed intensive monitoring.

'We'll keep her intubated for at least twenty-four hours. I want to be called if any of her parameters change, especially her blood pressure. I'm going to go and grab something to eat now, but I'll be staying here overnight.'

He'd half expected to see Evie hanging around the unit, waiting for news about how the surgery had gone. It was a relief she wasn't at her desk, he told himself as he finally headed to the cafeteria to find his first meal since breakfast. So why did he feel curiously let down? As if Evie had given up on Grace despite how involved she'd been with the baby ever since they'd found her?

And then he saw her through an open door, sitting alone in one of the family rooms. She saw him, too, but she didn't move. She looked pale and utterly miserable.

He couldn't simply walk past, could he?

Ryan stopped at the door.

'It's okay,' he said quietly. 'She's okay. The surgery went very well.'

Evie jumped to her feet and then burst into tears and threw herself at him. There was nothing he could do but open his arms to catch her. And then hold her until her sobs subsided.

It was Evie who pushed herself away.

'Sorry,' she said. 'I didn't mean to do that.' She swiped at the moisture on her face. 'You're right, you know.'

One side of his mouth curled into a smile. 'About?'

'Not getting involved. Staying away from cuddles. If it makes this sort of thing so hard for me, it would be impossible for you.' Evie pressed her fingers against trembling lips and then took a step back. 'Thank you,' she said. 'That was all I needed to hear. I can go home now.'

Ryan opened his mouth to ask her to stay. To talk to her about what had happened last night. To reassure her that it wasn't anything about her that meant that it couldn't go any further, it was *his* problem.

But any words got stuck on that lump in his throat and his view of Evie disappearing into the elevator was oddly blurry. He'd never reacted to the aftermath of the adrenaline rush of intricate surgery like this. He couldn't blame his weariness, either.

He'd changed, hadn't he?

Evie had changed him.

On the positive side, he had his answer to that question now so he'd never have to waste time wondering in the future. He wasn't some kind of monster. He *was* capable of that kind of emotional involvement. On the negative side, he had to find a way to shut it down again, as successfully as he had done for so many years.

He had to do it, for the sake of everybody involved. Especially Evie. He'd hurt her enough already. To do any more damage would be unforgiveable.

CHAPTER EIGHT

'You okay, Evie?'

'I'm fine, thanks, Janine.' Evie was keeping an eye on the man who was restocking the automatic drinks machine in the reception area. 'I'm looking forward to getting a hot chocolate. We ran out a couple of days ago.'

'Hmm…' Janine didn't look convinced by the tight smile she'd received. 'I'm sorry that we don't have anybody needing cuddles at the moment. Seems like everyone's got their mum close by.'

Evie just nodded as she swallowed the lump in her throat. She could do with a cuddle herself but she couldn't tell her friend that, could she? And this was all her own fault. She'd known it was a bad idea to date a colleague. She'd been tricked into it by Ryan's assurance that it wasn't really a date but who went out with a friend and ended up in bed with them? In *love* with them…

Who dabbled with a fantasy that turned into reality only to crumble into dust and didn't get hurt by it?

She'd barely seen Ryan since baby Grace's surgery a few days ago. Since she had fallen into his arms after that terrifying wait to find out if the surgery had been successful. He hadn't stopped by her desk to say hello, even, let alone have a chat. She avoided meeting his gaze if she could but, on the odd occasion it had happened, there was nothing significant in the eye contact. They would both nod and smile—as if they were just another member of staff at Hope Hospital. Like Marco, perhaps. Or Naomi.

'I'm pretty busy, anyway,' she told Janine. 'I got roped into that committee for planning the children's Christmas party. We've got our first meeting at five this afternoon, in fact.'

'You'll do a brilliant job.' Janine smiled. 'I'm going to make sure I'm on duty for the party. And for Christmas Day, if I can. I love trying to make it special for all the children stuck in here—and their families. Are we going to have a tree out here in Reception?'

'I'm sure we will,' Evie promised. 'All the wards are getting one and we can't have them in the ICU so we'd better do something amazing out here. We get a lot of children having to wait here with friends or relatives while their parents visit their siblings. Which reminds me, I want to put a call out to get some new toys in the box. Maybe I can ask Theo if I can get some funds for some new ones.'

'Don't ask him today,' Janine advised. 'I've heard he's bringing Ivy in for some tests. She's been unwell long enough for him to be getting really worried.'

'Oh, no…he will be worried. She's all he's got after losing Ivy's mum.'

'I know.' Janine frowned but then brightened. 'I do have some good news, though. Grace is looking better.

We were concerned after we took her off the ventilator because her blood pressure was too high but she's responded to the medication well.' She smiled at Evie. 'Just between you and me, I think you'll be allowed a cuddle very soon. Maybe tomorrow, even.'

Evie returned the smile but it faded the moment Janine turned away to head back into the unit.

She wanted that cuddle with Grace desperately enough for it to be a warning that it wasn't a good idea, any more than it had been a good idea to have that night with Ryan. She was too attached. Grace had come through her surgery and was now well on the way to recovery. There would be no more reason to keep her here as a patient and there hadn't been any response to the public appeal for her mother to come forward. Social Services would step in, maybe as early as next week, and find a foster home for the abandoned baby. Evie would never see her again and the thought was unbearable.

The committee meeting about the children's Christmas party was a lively one due to the enthusiasm of everybody involved. Some suggestions were tried and true, like having a Father Christmas distributing gifts from his sack to every small patient, carol singers and celebrities visiting the wards. Others were a little more impractical, such as a snow machine and chocolate fountain.

It was well after six p.m. by the time Evie returned to her desk to collect her coat and bag. Susie was waiting to enter the elevator as the doors opened for Evie.

'Oh... I was hoping to catch you but I'd thought

you'd left already.' Susie smiled. 'Janine tells me you're having withdrawal symptoms. If you're quick, you'll be able to feed Grace. She's well enough to be cuddled now.'

Evie hesitated. Fought and won the brief battle in her head and heart. 'Maybe another time,' she said. 'I should probably head home.'

'That's a shame.' The doors were closing on Susie. 'I think she's missing you.'

The battle lines had just been redrawn and this time Evie knew she had no chance of winning. Did Grace really recognise her? Was it possible that she could be feeling abandoned for the second time? A quick call home to let her family know that she would be late and an equally rapid dash to the changing room and, minutes later, Evie was in the unit, heading for Grace's corner. She was almost too late. A nurse had picked Grace up and was about to sit down and settle into feeding her. Then she saw Evie.

'Ah... Susie found you. That's great. Come and sit down, Evie. I bet Grace has been missing this as much as you have. And thank you,' she added as she put the baby into Evie's arms. 'I'd love to have sat with her for a while but we've got some really sick littlies in here at the moment and there's so much to do.'

'No problem,' Evie said, even though her heart was racing and she actually felt a little bit sick.

The familiar feel of this particular baby in her arms, the sound of her whimpers, the *smell* of her, even, was almost too much. There was no way that Grace could have been missing this as much as she had been. She pressed a soft kiss to that wispy hair.

She loved this baby so much. She loved being with all the babies she cuddled in here but Grace was more than just special. As she latched onto the teat, she was looking up at Evie as if she really did recognise her. As if, finally, everything was right in her small world.

Something her sister Stella had said popped into Evie's head.

'You like babies. Maybe you could look after her? The way you used to look after us when we were little...'

As if that was remotely possible.

But there was an echo of another voice there as well.

'You could do anything you want to do. Be anything that you want to be...'

They did pay foster parents, didn't they? Would it be enough? Maybe she should ask to talk to the people in Social Services. But would raising another child be what she wanted to devote her life to doing, now that her siblings were old enough to cope without her and she'd had a glimpse of a very different kind of future?

Evie looked around her, at the staff moving quietly in their tasks. At one nurse who was helping a mother change her baby's nappy and another who was beside another mother, holding her hand as she spoke to her. How could Evie do something that would take her away from this place?

Instead of talking to Social Services, maybe she should talk to a different group of people. Find out if her past studies could be built on and whether she could go back and finish her nursing degree in a shorter amount of time. Look into what it would take to become a specialist paediatric nurse and that way she would never have to leave a place like this to go and sit behind a desk or attend another committee meeting. She wouldn't have to stay away from babies because they were too sick or they had their own mothers helping to look after them.

Yes...that was what she really wanted, Evie decided. And she was going to do something about it. Tomorrow.

That decision, along with the joy of holding Grace as the baby fell asleep in her arms, was enough to lift Evie's spirits for the first time in days. Maybe the heartache of being pushed away by Ryan and the pain still to come from saying goodbye to Grace would be worth it in the end. If none of it had happened, she might never have taken this step forward in her life.

There were other steps being taken forward as Evie sat there having these thoughts but there was nowhere for her to hide as Ryan came towards her. He was wearing scrubs, as if he'd come straight from Theatre, and he looked as if it had been a difficult session. There were lines around his eyes that suggested a fierce focus on something for a long time, his jaw was shadowed by stubble and he had hat hair but he'd never looked more gorgeous.

Evie's heart rate picked up again and stumbled and there was an ache in her chest that told her this was too hard. It was true that, one day, she might be very grateful that he had come into her life and made her believe in herself again but it was too soon right now and it was just *too* hard to be this close to him.

'I'm just leaving,' she said hurriedly, before Ryan had a chance to say anything. 'Grace has finished her feed and I need to put her back to bed. Could you ask one of the nurses to help me, please? I don't want to hurt her.'

'She's fine,' Ryan said. 'But here…let me help.'

Evie opened her mouth to refuse, remembering the way he'd looked when she'd offered to hand Grace to him that time. As if holding her was the last thing he would ever want to do. And the way he had wrenched the baby from her arms the last time she'd been holding Grace. Even worse, the very first time he had helped her put Grace back into the incubator and the way the brush of his hands on her own body had triggered such an extraordinary awareness of him. Given her new knowledge of what those hands were capable of, the reminder of their lovemaking could well be the last straw as far as keeping her composure went.

But Ryan's hands were already there, large enough to support the tiny baby completely as he lifted her. And he didn't just turn and put her into her crib instantly. To Evie's astonishment, he kept hold of Grace, using his foot to pull another chair close and then sinking onto it, holding the baby tucked into the crook of one arm.

How weird was this?

He'd never simply held a baby when it had nothing to do with examining or treating them.

Evie clearly sensed that this was significant. She also looked more vulnerable than Ryan had ever seen her look. Scared, even, as if he was about to do something that might hurt her.

In fact, his intentions were the opposite. And it felt

right to be doing this here, like this. It was partly because he wanted to make up for the way he'd reacted
that time that Evie had offered him a cuddle with Grace
and he'd experienced that intense longing for what he'd
thought he never wanted—a family of his own. So, this
was a kind of test to see if he'd put that longing where
it belonged—too far away to be a problem ever again.

More than that, he wanted to try and turn back time
to when he and Evie were friends and his only intention had been to help her get more from her life. What
better way than to be holding the tiny person that had
brought them together in the first place?

'She's doing really well, our Gracie,' he said quietly.
'And a lot of that is down to you, Evie.'

'Hardly.' Evie was focused on the baby and didn't
look up to meet his gaze. 'You're the one who's saved
her life.'

'I might not have had the chance to do that if you
hadn't heard her that night out in the car park. She
might well have died if she'd been left there all night.
And you're the person who's given her something just
as important as any of her medical treatment. You've
given her so much time. And love. Her condition could
have been a lot more fragile going into surgery if it
hadn't been for you.'

'Thanks.' Evie's cheeks had gone bright pink.

'You're a born mother, aren't you? What you've
done for Grace. And for so many other babies here,
from what I've heard. What you've done for your own
brothers and sisters…it's extraordinary. *You're* extraordinary, Evie.'

He could see the way she was pressing her lips together, as if she was trying not to cry. He didn't want to make her cry. What he wanted to do at this moment was to take her into his arms and hold her so maybe it was just as well that he had his arms full of a baby.

'I can't imagine you without a family in your future,' he continued quietly. 'And that's why I could never be a part of that future. I wanted you to know that. Not to think that it has anything to do with who *you* are. You're gorgeous. Smart and warm and loving and there's someone out there who will be perfect for you. It just can't be me.'

'I don't understand.'

Evie's eyes were shimmering with unshed tears as she looked at him and her voice was no more than a whisper. A nurse gave them a curious glance but kept walking past. Maybe she thought they were talking about Grace's future prognosis or something. It was odd that they could be having such a private conversation in a space like this but, again, it felt like the right place.

'I had a little brother,' he told Evie. 'Jack. He was a few years younger than me and my dad died while Mum was pregnant with him so he was the best thing that happened in a pretty miserable time for her. He was certainly the most important thing in the world for my mother even before he was born and she was devastated to find out that he had some major abnormalities with his heart.'

'Oh, no...' A tear escaped Evie's eye and she reached out to touch Grace's little starfish hand that was poking out from her blanket. 'Just like Grace...'

'Worse than Grace. He was never going to survive for long.'

'Oh...' There was a world of compassion in that sound. 'That must have been so hard for you.'

Ryan swallowed hard. Nobody had ever focused on what it had been like for him. They'd been sorry for Jack and even more so for his mother but he'd just been a small child and maybe they'd all assumed that he was too young to be affected.

'Why do you say that?'

'Because sometimes kids get forgotten when someone else needs so much attention. And they don't understand. They can blame themselves for bad things that happen. Stella went through that when Mum died. She thought it was her fault because she'd been naughty.'

Ryan nodded slowly. 'I'm not sure that I blamed myself but I knew that Mum blamed me for being alive when Jack wasn't. I *was* too young to understand what depression was. I just learned that, no matter how hard I tried, I was never going to be special like Jack had been. And that it was better to just stay away from people because if you didn't try and make them love you, you didn't get hurt so much.'

'Oh... *Ryan*...that's the saddest thing I've ever heard.' Evie shook her head. 'Did you ever tell her how you felt?

'No.' Ryan shook his head. 'At first I didn't know how to. And then maybe I was scared that it would only make it worse because it would confirm my fears. Finally, it just became the invisible elephant in the room.'

He didn't want Evie to feel sorry for him. It was all ancient history now.

'It got easier,' he said. 'I got sent away to boarding school. I discovered that sports were a great way to burn off emotional stuff that got in the way. And then I got to medical school and by then I'd added sex into my repertoire of physical therapy.' He offered Evie a small smile. 'I'm not proud of myself. I'm only telling you this so you can understand why the idea of family, or getting really close to someone, isn't an option for me. I just couldn't go there. I've perfected my ability to keep a distance and it works. It works for what I do for a job, too. I couldn't do what I do if I got too close to my patients.'

He wasn't blaming Evie for getting too involved with this particular baby but it was going to be very hard for her when they took Grace away. He remembered holding her while she had been sobbing after her agonising wait to hear how the surgery had gone. Maybe she could learn from this experience—from him—and keep more of a distance herself in future.

Evie dropped her gaze to the baby in his arms and then looked up at him again. She didn't need to say anything—it was blatantly obvious that he was doing something that wasn't in his rule book.

'Yeah... I know. You've rubbed off on me. It's not something I'm going to make a habit of, but I think you've made me a bit more human. And...and I'm hoping that we can still be friends?'

'Friends,' Evie echoed. There was a note in her voice that made Ryan think of someone thanking someone else for a gift that they really didn't want. But then she smiled at him and her tone was brighter. Casual, even.

'Sure,' she said as she got to her feet. 'Friends it is. I've really got to get going, though. My family will be wondering where on earth I've got to.' She leaned down to stroke her finger over Grace's head. 'Sleep tight, button,' she murmured. 'I'll be in early to give you your breakfast.' She turned away without meeting his gaze. 'See you later, Ryan.'

It was a good thing that Evie was going home to a house that was full of people. Okay, it was full of mess and arguments and being taken for granted but there was a lot of love there that just got a bit buried under everyday life. She would far rather have that than to be going home to a beautiful but lonely penthouse apartment.

But maybe Ryan had also taught himself to never be lonely?

Evie's heart had broken for the little boy that Ryan Walker had been. She couldn't imagine what it must have been like to have felt so unloved. She could understand why he believed that it was better to keep a distance from people. She'd even thought that herself, when she'd realised that she was far too attached to baby Grace, but she couldn't be someone other than herself and the pain was worth it for the joy that was the other side of the coin of being so involved.

Her heart was breaking for the man that Ryan Walker had become, as well, because he was never going to know that kind of joy. Maybe keeping an emotional distance did make him a better surgeon but at what price? He deserved to know what it was like to love. To be loved.

Her heart was also breaking for herself, because she wasn't going to be the person who could teach him that he was wrong. That there were more important things in life than being the best in the world at your profession.

But she knew she couldn't be anything other than herself.

And probably Ryan couldn't either.

CHAPTER NINE

HIS FEET WERE already pounding the pathway in a steady, fast rhythm but Ryan pushed his speed even further, until his lungs were burning with the effort. It was too dark and miserable with an icy rain falling for anybody else to be using these paths along The Backs yet and that suited him just fine.

He didn't want company. And the miserable weather was just an echo of what had filled his heart and woken him so early to find the shocking remnants of tears on his face.

Maybe he shouldn't have opened his heart to Evie yesterday. He'd never spoken of his childhood to anybody and it had unlocked something that had come back to haunt his dreams. Or, more likely, it was the fact that Evie had understood something that nobody else ever had that had taken him back so vividly.

He'd been a small child again. Feeling worthless because he wasn't loved. Knowing that he wasn't good enough. Because he wasn't Jack... Fighting so hard to try and win his mother's attention and working so hard at school because he thought that if she was proud of him, maybe that would be enough. Somewhere, in

the dream, his adult self was watching that child—
telling him to stop trying because it would never happen. Promising that, if he could shut himself so far
away that it didn't matter how others felt about him,
the pain would go away.

It was astonishing how real pain could be in a
dream. Enough for the ache to still be there after he'd
pulled himself from his bed and come out here to purge
any remaining emotional disturbance by replacing it
with enough physical exertion to provide the kind of
pain that was so much easier to deal with.

What a valuable lesson it had been, way back then,
to discover that you could harness negative emotions to
push yourself into achieving things you might not have
thought you were capable of. And running had been the
first sport Ryan had excelled at. Maybe his mother had
never been there to cheer him on in his school races but
his own pride in his achievement, even more than the
applause of others, had been enough. By the time he
was at boarding school, he was ready to push himself
academically as well. He'd given up trying to win his
mother's love by then. Now it was all about proving
to himself that he was worthwhile. That he deserved
to be the child who had survived.

The lights in the grounds of the University of Cambridge made it easy to recognise the landmark. This
was where Evie's brother had fallen off his bike. Where
he'd had a glimpse of the kind of bonds that she had
with her family. Bonds that had been holding her back,
perhaps, but they were people she loved who must love
her back. Who wouldn't love Evie?

He hated that he'd hurt her. He hadn't meant to.

He should never have let himself get carried away that night and make love to her but he had lacked the strength to resist and now he felt ashamed of himself. With a grunt of pain, Ryan pushed himself even harder, until he'd left that particular stretch of track far enough behind to escape the thoughts about Evie. Until the only thing he was aware of was the punishment his muscles and lungs and heart were having to cope with.

Any fragments of those dreams were being left even further behind.

He could win this battle. Like he had learned to do so long ago.

'I don't want to go to school. I feel sick.' Stella pulled her bed covers over her head. 'Go away, Evie.'

Evie walked further into her sister's room. 'What kind of sick?'

'I don't know...' The grumble was muffled. 'Just sick.'

Evie pulled back the covers far enough to feel Stella's forehead. 'You're not running a temperature and you don't sound like you've got a cold, so what's going on?'

Stella wrenched the covers back. 'My stomach hurts, okay?'

'Oh...' Evie nodded. 'Is it your period?'

Stella said nothing.

'How 'bout I bring you a cup of tea and some paracetamol? Then you can get up and have breakfast and see how you feel.' She paused at the door. 'Sometimes we've just got to get on with stuff, even if we don't feel great. It's part of growing up.'

Evie wasn't feeling great herself. Funny how dealing with difficult emotional things could actually feel like there was something physically wrong. Her stomach hurt, too. Or maybe it was the ache around her heart that had just expanded.

She knocked on her brother's door. 'Bobby? Time to get up.'

There was no point in knocking on Peter's door. He had been quite old enough to get himself up and away to school for a long time now.

Going down to the kitchen, Evie set out cereal boxes on the table while the kettle boiled to make tea but then she pulled a pot from the cupboard. It was a miserable, rainy morning and maybe some hot porridge would give them all a better start. It was starting to look un-likely that she would get away early enough to be able to give Grace a bottle before she was due to start work.

Her father had the television on in the living room.

'Anything happening in the world I should know about?' Evie called as she went past with Stella's mug of tea and paracetamol.

He didn't answer so she carried on up the stairs. Bobby stumbled past sleepily, heading downstairs. The tea in the mug sloshed onto Stella's bedside table when Evie heard him yelling, moments later.

'Evie… *Evie*…come quick. It's Dad…'

Her father was slumped onto one end of the couch.

'Dad?' She shook his shoulder. *'Dad?'*

A glance at the coffee table showed that he had re-cently given himself an injection of insulin but where was his blood glucose monitor? Had he even checked the level of his blood sugar before he'd dosed himself with medication to lower it?

'Bobby…find me Dad's testing kit. It's probably in the kitchen.'

Her father's skin was cold and clammy and his pulse was racing. He'd had episodes of low blood sugar in the past but usually the symptoms were obvious much earlier, with confusion or dizziness, and they were easy enough to manage with a sugar hit like jellybeans. He wasn't conscious enough to eat anything now, though.

Bobby came running back with the small case that held the monitor, testing strips and lancets but Evie sent him straight back to the kitchen.

'Get me the jar of honey that's on the table.'

Bobby was looking frightened. 'Is Dad going to die?'

'No, love. He's just got a really low blood sugar level. I know what to do.'

Peter appeared in the doorway as Evie pricked her father's finger and transferred the drop of blood to the test strip she had slotted into the monitor. 'I've called an ambulance,' he told her. 'They're on their way.'

Stella was right behind him. 'What's happened?'

'I don't know. Maybe Dad didn't eat enough last night. Or he could be unwell. Sometimes insulin doses are difficult to manage and it looks like he's had too much this morning.' The level on the strip was too low to give any figures on the monitor screen. It simply had the letters 'Lo'.

'It's your fault.' Stella was crying now. 'You weren't here to see what he had for dinner. You're *never* here these days…'

'That's not true.' Evie stuck her finger into the jar of honey and then rubbed it onto her father's gums.

There was some truth in the accusation, though. She had been late last night, staying after that meeting to be with Grace. And Ryan... She'd been absent far more often ever since the night that Grace had been found. Ever since she'd met Ryan.

Paramedics arrived and took over with impressive efficiency.

'We'll get a line in and give him some IV glucose.' One of the team smiled at her. 'It'll work a lot faster than the honey.'

She watched them slip a cannula into a vein in her dad's forearm and attach a line and bag of fluid. They also put ECG dots on his chest and wrapped a blood pressure cuff around his arm. Even as they got their first measurements, her father was stirring and opening his eyes.

'This is one of my favourite jobs,' the paramedic told his audience of Evie and all her siblings. 'It's like magic, how fast it works.'

Her father blinked slowly and took in the scene around him. And then he groaned.

'Oh, no...'

The paramedic was holding his finger. 'Small jab, sir. Let's see how your level's looking now.'

Evie caught her father's gaze. 'You didn't test it, did you? Before you gave yourself your injection.'

He shook his head. 'I couldn't remember where I'd left the kit.'

'He might have already had a low level,' the paramedic suggested. 'And a bit of confusion.' He looked at the monitor he was holding. 'Still low but he's conscious enough to eat now. We'll finish this glucose infusion but he'll need some complex carbohydrates, maybe a cheese sandwich, to follow it up or he might go back into a hypo.'

'Does he need to go into hospital?'

'Not if there's someone who can stay with him and keep a close eye on his sugar level for a few hours at least.'

Evie nodded. 'I can do that. I'll ring and let them know I won't be coming in today.'

'I'm sorry, Evie.' Her father rubbed his forehead. 'I should be better at managing this myself by now.'

'I could stay with him,' Peter offered.

'And me,' Stella added. 'I was going to stay home, anyway.'

Evie shook her head. 'You've both got exams on at the moment. It's important that you get to school. Bobby? You need to go and get dressed.'

But Bobby was crouched beside the defibrillator, watching the pattern of his father's heart rhythm on the screen.

'This is *so* cool,' he said. 'I wanna be a paramedic when I grow up.'

The female paramedic ruffled his hair. 'Then you need to go to school, mate. And work hard. Go and get dressed. I'll let you help me take your dad's blood pressure when you come back again.'

By the time the medical team packed up their gear and left, Evie's father was on his feet. And very apologetic.

'It was stupid. It won't happen again.'

'Let's get some food into you, Dad. How 'bout some cheese toasties instead of a sandwich? Maybe some porridge, too.'

Evie went back into the kitchen. Her movements, as she prepared the hot food, felt wooden, however. Automatic. This was what she did, wasn't it? She took care of her family. Had it only been yesterday that she'd decided so firmly that she would follow her own dreams and go back to finish her nursing training?

It felt like that dream was crumbling into nothing, like an echo of that fantasy of being more than a 'friend' to Ryan Walker.

'Where's Evie this morning?'

Ryan hadn't expected to see her at her desk this early but now he'd discovered that she wasn't in the unit with baby Grace, either.

'She's going to be late,' Janine told him. 'If she gets here at all today. Her father apparently had a hypoglycaemic crisis earlier this morning. She needs to stay with him until she's sure he's stable.'

Of course she did. Family came first to Evie, didn't it?

'I'm just doing a quick check on my patients here to make sure no complications are cropping up. I'll be tied up in Theatre all day and here overnight as well. This one's going to need careful watching after her surgery today.'

'Oh? Who is she? I haven't got a post-surgery admission flagged for today.'

'No. She's going next door. She's ten months old so doesn't qualify for neonatal admission.'

'But she does qualify for a neonatal surgeon?'

'It's a complex surgery that I've had experience with. A double switch.'

Janine's eyes widened. 'Wow...that's rare.'

'It is. And a first for Hope Hospital. Theo asked me to take the case.'

'Good luck. Hey...did Theo mention anything about Ivy? I've heard he's really concerned that nothing's been pinpointed as the reason she's unwell.'

'He did say something about it being a shame that some expert diagnostician from the States couldn't come earlier than planned. Someone called Madison Archer. Have you heard of her?'

Janine shook her head. 'There's been a push to get international experts here, though.' She smiled at Ryan. 'Like you. Are you glad you came?'

'Of course.'

He was glad, he told himself as he headed to the theatre suite for possibly the biggest challenge he would face for a long time. As he arrived, he found baby Gemma in her mother's arms, her father beside them, as they waited outside the induction area.

Gemma had been born with dextracardia, which meant her heart pointed to the right side of her chest instead of the left. She also had life-threatening complications with the major veins and arteries of the heart joined to the wrong chambers. She had had a previous surgery when only a few months old as a temporary measure but this major procedure would mean that her heart would be able to function far more normally.

'All set?' He smiled at Gemma's parents.

'Scared stiff,' the mother admitted, hugging her daughter tightly.

Gemma's father cleared his throat. 'It's going to be okay, isn't it?'

'It's going to be a long day,' Ryan warned.

He could feel their fear. Imagine them sitting in a private room somewhere nearby for the agonising wait of hearing how the surgery had gone. The way Evie had been sitting waiting for news of Grace, except she had done that by herself. How strong had she been to cope with that?

He could still remember the shape of Evie's body in his arms as she'd sobbed with relief. Could still hear the echo of her voice telling him he was right. That it was better not to get too involved with patients because it would make it impossible for him to do what he had to do. He'd told himself that so often and it was true.

'We'll make sure you get updates at every stage of the surgery,' he told Gemma's parents. 'And we'll be taking the very best care of her, I promise.'

His own words were still in his head as he walked towards the operating table a short time later. The baby had been anaesthetised and draped so all he should be aware of was the small window in the sterile drapes that exposed the chest.

But he was aware of the shape of the whole baby lying on this table. Of seeing her in the arms of the people who loved her so much. Of just how much was riding on him being able to achieve what he'd promised he could. Maybe that was why, when he picked up a scalpel, he could feel a tiny tremor in his fingers that would have been invisible to anyone else but was enough to be a warning that Ryan had no intention of ignoring.

Okay…he had changed. He knew he was capable of feelings that he'd believed he had excised from his life but he could control them even if it might be the hardest thing he ever had to do.

He *had* to. This was who he was. Who he would always be.

It was the latest Evie had been at work since the night of the gala. The first time she had ever given Grace her late-night feed and helped settle her for the night.

'Thanks, Evie,' one of the nurses at the central station said as she left. 'You're so good with Grace.'

'She's adorable.' Evie smiled. 'It's a joy to spend time with her.' She reached for a few empty coffee mugs littering the desk. 'I'll take those back to the staffroom. I'm heading that way to get changed.'

The staffroom and departmental library were just beyond the changing rooms and showers. The night lighting was softer and Evie almost missed the figure sprawled on one of the comfortable couches that lined three sides of the space, around a large central table and the workspace with the fridge and dishwasher and microwave oven.

'Evie…what on earth are you doing here at this time of night?'

'Long story…' Evie headed for the bench to rinse the mugs and put them into the dishwasher. Her heart was thumping. This was harder than she'd thought it would be but it felt oddly intimate, being alone in a room with Ryan, late at night. Intimate and…sad…

'How's your dad?'

Her head swivelled. 'How did you know about that?'

Ryan's smile was crooked. 'You weren't here this morning, so I asked. Janine filled me in.'

'Oh...' He'd noticed she wasn't there? He'd been concerned enough to find out why, in case she wasn't well or something?

He did care, even if it was only as a friend. Evie blinked back the prickle that could have turned into tears but the ache around her heart was receding. A friendship wasn't something to be thrown away just because it was less than what she really wanted. She couldn't walk away from this opportunity to be this close to him, either. The pull was too strong. She cared too much and she could see the deep lines of weariness in Ryan's face. The almost grim set of his mouth when his half-smile faded.

Evie looked down at the rinsed mugs in her hands. 'Do you want a coffee?'

'No. I've had a long session in Theatre. I'm still a bit too wired for any more coffee.'

She turned away, fighting the impression that she was being rejected along with a hot drink.

'A hot chocolate would be great, though. Have one with me?'

'Sure.' Oh...was it pathetic to feel a rush of pleasure at the request? Hope, even? Not that this was going to be the start of something new between them. Or maybe it was. The start of a friendship, perhaps. Where they both recognised the boundaries that couldn't be crossed but they could still enjoy each other's company?

Ryan moved to sit at the central table as Evie prepared the drinks.

'So, what's this long story?' he asked.

'Well… Dad had the hypo this morning. I don't think he'd had enough dinner last night and he didn't bother checking his BGL before he gave himself his morning dose of insulin. Bobby found him unconscious in front of the TV. I was using honey on his gums to try and get him to absorb some sugar but Pete called an ambulance and they gave him a glucose infusion.'

'Sounds like it gave you all a fright.'

'Yeah…' Evie put a mug in front of Ryan and sat down at the table beside him. 'It was a bit fraught. My sister, Stella, told me it was all my fault.'

'What?' Ryan shook his head. 'How did she come to that conclusion?'

'Because I wasn't there to see how much Dad ate last night. And I didn't remind him to check his level this morning, I guess. I don't know… When you're fourteen, it's easy to lash out and blame someone.'

'Hardly fair.' His gaze caught Evie's. 'After all you've done for them for all these years. You deserve a break.'

The look in his eyes reminded Evie so much of when they'd stopped to talk on their way home from the ball. When he'd been telling her this for the first time—that she'd done such an amazing job for her family. That it was time she started chasing her own dreams. That she could be anything she wanted to be.

The time just before he'd kissed her…

She had to break the eye contact so she stared at the chocolate streaks on the foam topping her mug.

'I think it's been a positive thing,' she told him quietly. 'I had a lot of time to talk to Dad while I stayed home to watch him and tonight, when everyone was there for dinner, he told us that things were going to be different from now on.'

'What did he say?'

'That it was his fault that he got sick this morning because he hadn't taken enough responsibility for his own health because it was too easy to rely on me. That he'd been doing that ever since Mum died and it wasn't fair.'

Ryan nodded approvingly.

'He told them that I'd given up far more than they realised to look after them all. That I should have been a nurse. That maybe I should be able to have a life of my own as well.'

'How did your brothers and sister react to that?'

'Amazingly well,' Evie said. 'Probably thanks to you.'

Ryan gave a huff of laughter. 'I doubt that.'

'No. It's true. They were all a bit astonished that night I went to the ball with you. It was the first time they'd seen me really dressed up and Stella had been excited to help me do my hair and make-up. I think it was the first time they saw me as someone more than their substitute mother to get dinner on the table and clean clothes ready to wear.'

'In that case, I'm really glad I asked you.'

'Me, too.'

There was a silence then as they both sipped their drinks. Was Ryan thinking the same thing that Evie was? That she was glad that night had ended the way it had? Because otherwise she might never have known what it was like to be with someone that you were in love with. That sex could be so much more amazing than she would ever have believed. Maybe it was going to be a hard ask to find anyone who could give her what Ryan had given her but she wasn't going to settle for anything less. Ever.

Ryan cleared his throat. 'So, what's the plan, then?'

'Dad's set up a roster. Household tasks are going to be shared. And then he asked me what it was I would do if I didn't have so much to do around the house and I told them I wanted to go back and finish my nursing training.'

Ryan's hand closed over Evie's on the table. 'That's fantastic.'

'Mmm.' The touch of his skin against hers was overwhelming but Evie didn't move her hand away. She couldn't. 'So that's why I'm here tonight. It was my family that suggested I come in for a while. When I was explaining why I wanted to be a nurse so much, I told them about Gracie and how much I loved her. That I'd even been wondering about fostering or adopting her.'

'Really?' Her hand felt suddenly cool as Ryan removed his touch, so astonished that he was rubbing his forehead. 'You'd really consider doing that?'

Evie shook her head. 'I can't,' she said sadly. 'It wouldn't be fair on anyone and our house isn't big enough and that could mean that I'd never get the chance to finish my studies.' She offered Ryan a smile. 'One dream at a time, huh?'

He smiled back. 'Yeah…there's plenty of time for your other dreams. One day, you'll have a baby of your own to cuddle and they'll be the luckiest kid in the world.'

Oh…she couldn't go down that conversational route and talk about hypothetical children that would have a father who wouldn't be Ryan. Desperately, she searched for a way to change the subject.

'So why are you here so late, anyway?' She risked a quick glance, aware again of how exhausted he was looking.

'I only got out of surgery a little while ago and I need to stay around.'

'Was it an emergency?'

'No. It started this morning. Took a bit over twelve hours.'

Evie's jaw dropped. 'Goodness…what kind of surgery takes that long?'

'It's called a double switch.' Ryan searched Evie's gaze to gauge how interested she really was. He'd been going over every step of that complex surgery again in his head just before she'd come into the staffroom and a chance to talk about it was exactly what he needed. Not just as a debrief. It was far safer territory than talking about things like the family of her own that Evie would have one day. Maybe it was better for Evie, too. After all, she'd been the one to change the subject.

'Never heard of it. Sounds like a heart transplant.'

'It almost is, kind of. Except that you use the patient's own heart.' Yes, she was interested, all right. Fascinated, even? Ryan reached for the scrap paper that always sat in the middle of the table and pulled a pen from his tunic pocket.

'This little girl was born with dextracardia,' he said, drawing a shape on the paper. 'Meaning that the heart points to the right instead of the left. For Gemma, it also meant that everything else was messed up. Blood from the right atrium, here, was going into the left ventricle, here...' He drew arrows onto his diagram. 'And that meant that it was deoxygenated blood being sent to the rest of her body instead of to the lungs where it needed to go. What I had to do was detach the major arteries and veins and then reattach them to make the blood travel in the direction it's supposed to.'

'How old is Gemma?'

Ryan smiled. That was Evie all over, wasn't it? She had remembered the baby's name. She wanted to know about the small person who was having the surgery as much as any technical information. It made him want to touch her hand again. To kiss her... He actually had to drag his gaze away from her face. From her lips. And it left a curious ache in his chest.

'Ten months,' he said crisply. 'They picked up the problem when she was only about two months old so she had an operation then to put a band around her pulmonary artery and limit the amount of oxygenated blood that was getting sent back to the lungs. She needed to be a bit older so that there was a bit more space to work with for the major procedure. Plus, she needed to be stronger to get through such a long time on bypass.'

'Is she going to be all right?'

'Everything's looking good at the moment. Her parents are in PICU, sitting beside her bed, but it'll be a couple of days before we can take her off the ventilator.'

'They must be so relieved that it's over.'

Ryan nodded but what he was really thinking about was the empathy Evie had for a patient's relatives as much as for the patient themselves, and that was a big part of working in paediatrics.

'You're going to be such a brilliant nurse,' he told her. 'Or a doctor, for that matter. Maybe you'll get so inspired by your training, you won't want to stop.'

Evie made a face. 'I couldn't do what you do,' she said. 'At least, with nursing, you can get a bit closer to your patients. Cuddle them, even.'

Ryan swallowed the last of his hot chocolate. It was on the tip of his tongue to tell Evie that he'd almost wobbled today. That his focus had been fuzzy around the edges because he'd seen his patient as a small person on that operating table and not just a small window of chest that had to be opened. That it was Evie who'd changed his perception.

But that wasn't something positive, like the way his invitation to a ball had altered her family's perception of Evie. She might see it as something negative. That she had made his job more difficult. And that might make her back off from even a friendship with him.

Ryan didn't want that to happen. However hard it might be to spend time with Evie and keep his distance, he knew that the difference she was making to his life was important.

That she was very, very special.

He could keep his emotional distance because he was determined not to hurt her again. Giving up the chance to spend time in her company was asking too much but there was a limit to how much he could cope with in one go.

'I'd better go and check on her,' he said, pushing his chair back. 'Thanks for the chocolate.'

'Anytime.' Evie picked up the empty mugs.

Ryan turned his head as he went out the door. Just for another glimpse of Evie as she stood at the sink, rinsing the mugs. The light was catching her hair, making it glow like a halo, and that made him smile.

Yep. Evie Cooper could definitely qualify as an angel.

She *was* that special.

CHAPTER TEN

IT WAS EVIE'S FAULT.

Ryan shrugged off his coat, draped it over one of the chairs at his dining table and looked around his apartment with a sinking feeling.

He hated this space.

It was too big. Too minimal. Way too empty.

The bedroom was the worst space because he couldn't glimpse that bed without remembering Evie being in it. Maybe it had only been for a few hours but it had changed everything.

For the first time in his life, Ryan was lonely.

And, also for the first time, he realised that he had been lonely for his entire life.

That was down to Evie as well because what was happening between them now was possibly the first *real* friendship he'd ever experienced. It wasn't that he didn't have plenty of people he counted as friends, it was just that there was something much more to his relationship with Evie now. How could there not be, when the attraction was still there, even if they were both successfully staying within the boundaries that he had set so firmly?

That late-night conversation in the staffroom had given Ryan exactly what he wanted—a return to the way it had been before he'd made the mistake of getting too close to Evie. They were talking again. Snatching any available moments to spend a few minutes together, whether it was at the reception area desk, in the staffroom, or beside Grace's bed.

He had actually shared Evie's mixed feelings when little Grace caught a cold and her recovery was set back somewhat. It was distressing to see the baby so uncomfortable with her blocked-up nose and cough and it was worrying that she was having difficulty feeding and her weight had dropped a little, but it also meant that there was no way they were going to discharge her too soon and that meant that Evie had more time to spend with the baby she loved so much.

She was following baby Gemma's progress with great interest now, as well. And she wanted to hear about every surgery that Ryan had done since then. She always had some scrap paper available so that he could draw pictures and illustrate his explanations of exactly what he did to repair little hearts. He had also put considerable effort into helping Evie write up an application for returning to her nursing degree and it had been his suggestion to add references from staff members here, even Theo Hawkwood, who'd smiled and said, 'If that's what you really want, Evie, I'll do whatever it takes to help.'

He'd looked rueful as well, however. 'You're going to be badly missed, Evie. No one else could have got that Christmas committee so completely on track and you've come up with some brilliant ideas. I hear you scored the last two giant trees that were available as well. You're a bit of a legend around here, you know.'

'She doesn't need to disappear for ever,' Ryan had said. 'I reckon she'll get cross-crediting for all her previous training. She might only need six to twelve months to complete her degree and then we could have her back as a nurse. How good would that be?'

Theo was nodding. And smiling. 'I can guarantee there'll be a job for you here from the day that you graduate.'

'I'd love to still be able to come in while I'm study-ing. Just for some cuddling duties.'

'We'll make that happen. I might even write up a job description and employ you for that, too.' Theo had shaken Evie's hand. 'Best of luck. If the powers-that-be don't snap up your application, they're idiots.'

Evie wasn't the only person delighted to know that she would still be welcome when she gave up her job at Reception. It meant that Ryan would still see her reg-ularly. He could help her with her studies. She might be able to help him, too, with what was becoming an increasing issue every time he came home from work.

'Any word?'

'I only posted the application yesterday.' Evie had her arms full of toys that she was putting back into one of the colourful baskets in the waiting area. 'I probably won't hear anything this side of Christmas.'

'Hmm…okay…well, I have a problem I hope you can help me with in the meantime.'

'Sure. What's that?'

Ryan followed Evie back to her desk. 'I hate my apartment.'

'Oh?'

'It's too... I don't know. Clean. It feels like a hotel, not a home.'

'I thought you like minimal and modern.'

'I do. Or I did.'

For some reason Ryan wasn't quite meeting Evie's gaze and it made her curious. Instinctively, she recognised that a boundary was too close and there was effort going on to stay on the right side of it. It was possible that Ryan wasn't even aware of it but she was getting familiar with the sensation as she tried to make this new friendship work. There were odd moments, like right now, when she noticed something like that frown line between Ryan's eyes and the urge to touch him was something she had to suppress very firmly. Or to say something that might be just too personal.

He wanted to live in a place that felt like home? That meant that he was feeling something that wasn't pleasant. Like loneliness? Had he ever actually lived in a place that felt like a real home? Evie tried to keep a wash of empathy from showing on her face.

'So you want to find a new apartment to rent?'

'No.' Ryan was silent for a moment, as if he was trying to figure out what he did want. 'I'm here to stay, Evie,' he said then. 'I think I want to buy something.'

'An apartment? Close to work?'

He shook his head. 'I think I want a house.'

That was a surprise. Why would someone who had vowed that a family, or simply a permanent partner, was no part of his future want to live in a house?

Because, maybe, he did want that kind of future, but he wasn't ready to admit it?

It had to be a good thing. A step towards what Evie would wish for the man she would probably love for the rest of her life. It might be a big ask, to help him find a home to share with someone who wasn't going to be her but she could do that. Like the way she could love a baby that she knew she was going to have to say goodbye to.

'Leave it with me,' she told Ryan. 'When I get a free moment, I'll trawl some property sites and see what's out there at the moment.'

'Thanks, Evie.' He gave her one of those smiles and Evie pressed her feet to the floor to try and stop its toe-curling effect. 'I knew I could count on you, mate.'

It was perhaps unfortunate that it was a relatively quiet day for the reception area team. Even Michelle got interested in what was currently on the local property market and more than one person who went past noticed that there was something unofficial on computer screens.

Naomi, the physiotherapist, had paused to say hello as she was on her way to visit a small patient in a nearby ward.

'Are you house hunting, Evie?'

'No. I'm just checking out what's available for one of our new doctors. Have you met Ryan Walker, our neonatal cardiac surgeon?'

'I did. At the gala.' Naomi smiled. 'I guess he'll be after a flash apartment? Something to impress?'

Ryan must have given the impression of being a playboy quite convincingly. Evie thought back to that night and that incident in the car park when she'd been knocked over by his glittering companion. When she'd noted the expensive sports car he'd arrived in. It wasn't surprising that he would have given that impression, was it, because that's who Ryan was to outward appearances.

It was only Evie who knew better.

The only person, possibly, who knew that a sad little boy was still hiding somewhere inside that confident surgeon.

But she abandoned the search after Naomi had gone. She hadn't been bookmarking or printing out the details of anything flashy. If she was honest, she'd been flagging the kind of place she would choose as a dream home and the idea of a succession of women being taken there for a one-night stand was suddenly rather distasteful.

Ryan could find his own house.

'This one.'

Evie shifted baby Grace to her shoulder and began rubbing her back. 'Where did you find those?' She could swear she'd put all those printed pages in the recycling box.

'Michelle left them for me in an envelope. And this is the one I want to have a look at.'

Oh, no… It was the barn conversion that had captured Evie completely. She could have kept that picture for herself, just to dream over occasionally.

'It's not anywhere near work. It would probably be a thirty-minute commute. And you could get snowed in during winter.'

'That's what they invented SUVs for, isn't it? And I can always stay here overnight if it's necessary.' Ryan had his eyebrows raised. 'What are you doing Saturday afternoon?'

'I don't know. Grocery shopping, probably. Or taking Bobby somewhere. I might even start some Christmas shopping. Why?'

'I want to make an appointment to see this place. And I need you to come with me.'

Wiping baby Grace's nose when she sneezed was a perfect excuse to take a moment of time before responding. To deal with that urge to do exactly that. To find out if it was possible that Ryan could fall in love with a house when he couldn't do it with a person. But how hard would that be?

'It's going to be your house, Ryan. You don't need me to help you decide what you want.'

'I do. You know stuff that I don't know. I've lived in apartments. Boarding schools. Hotels, even. I don't really know what I'm looking for here.'

'You'll know when you see it.'

'How?' Ryan looked bewildered.

'It's how it makes you feel,' Evie said quietly.

Looking up, she caught his gaze and something inside her melted. Ryan didn't do feelings like that. He didn't know how to so he really didn't know what he was doing. For whatever reason, he was stepping well out of his comfort zone here by entertaining the idea of choosing a living space on an emotional basis. And he was asking for her help.

How could she possibly resist that?

Her breath came out in a long sigh. 'Okay… I'll

come with you. But, are you sure you want to see this place? Michelle found some pretty spectacular apartments for sale.'

'No. This one.' Ryan was smiling at her again. 'I think I have a feeling about it already. I just want to be sure.'

The real estate agent was assuming they were a couple.

Of course she was. Was that why Evie had been reluctant to come with him on this excursion?

She didn't seem to be minding now. One glance at her face as they pulled up in the gravelled courtyard flanked by ancient brick buildings and he could see that she was enchanted. He loved the way her eyes shone and her cheeks went pink when she was excited about something. She couldn't be more of an opposite to him in that regard, given that he could hide his emotions so easily. Or was he losing that ability, along with the ability to not even feel them in the first place?

He could certainly feel something now. Ryan got out of the car and took in the square stone building with its brick inserts as an arch over the front door, blue shutters on the upper-storey windows and tall shutters folded back from French doors on the ground level. Joined on, and at a right angle was another long, low, stone building. The original stable doors had been kept, painted blue to match the shutters.

'This conversion has been done to the highest imaginable standards,' the real estate agent told them. 'Double glazing throughout, central heating and, while it's got every modern convenience inside, they've used recycled materials wherever possible to maintain period features.'

Evie loved the kitchen, with its flagged floor, a shiny new Aga oven and miles of gleaming granite work surfaces. The living room had a beamed ceiling and a massive fireplace.

'Oh… I could just see myself on one of those leather couches on a winter's night,' Ryan said. He grinned at her. 'Don't you just love an open fire?'

'Mmm…' As if that mattered when she wouldn't be here to enjoy it.

She followed them into one gorgeous bedroom after another, all with en suite bathrooms. There was an office and even a home gym that made Ryan smile even more.

Outside, there were tall trees that looked as old as the buildings and a paddock big enough to house ponies. The property was amazing but there was no way it could be considered a bachelor pad. It was a family home. Surely that vibe would have been enough to put Ryan off?

'I'm interested,' he told the estate agent. 'I'll sleep on it but it's quite likely I'm going to want to put in an offer.'

'Don't leave it too long,' the estate agent warned. 'Places like this, within easy commuting distance of Cambridge, get snapped up really fast.'

Dusk was falling as Ryan drove Evie back to where she'd left her car in the Hope Hospital car park.

'I felt it,' he told her. 'It felt like…home.'

'Not too big, then?'

He shrugged. 'I won't need to use all the rooms,

that's true. But that living room and kitchen—they were special, weren't they?'

'And you'd have time to mow the lawns?'

'I'm sure there's a local gardening company that could look after that.'

'And what about the paddock?' she couldn't resist teasing him. 'You planning to take up horse riding or something?'

Ryan laughed. 'I'll bet there are some little girls around who'd love to keep their ponies there. And isn't this village great? Look...' He waved a hand at the side window. 'That could be my local pub. We could do Sunday lunch there sometimes.'

'Sure.' Evie kept her tone noncommittal but the thought that he was thinking of her as part of this potential new life gave her a burst of pleasure that was hard to keep contained so that it didn't sprout into hope. The confirmation that she needed to protect herself came only moments later.

'But you're probably right,' Ryan muttered. 'I'd be rattling around by myself in a place like that. It would be crazy, wouldn't it? I don't know what I was thinking...'

They finished the trip in silence. When they got to the hospital, Ryan didn't bother driving right into the car park. He stopped near the barrier arm that was close to the ambulance bay and the bank of rubbish bins where they'd found Grace.

Where they'd shared their first kiss.

It was almost dark and the security lights would be coming on at any moment. If it hadn't become an automatic reaction to seeing those bins to take another look, it might have been difficult to spot something new that didn't seem to fit the scene.

'What's that?'

'What…where?'

'By the recycling bin. In the shadows. Look…it's… a person. A young girl.'

A girl who was standing very still. Hoping not to be noticed, perhaps?

'She's in the exact place that Grace was left,' Evie whispered. 'Are you thinking what I'm thinking?'

'That it's Grace's mother?' Ryan switched off the engine and reached for the handle of his door. 'I think we should find out, don't you?'

CHAPTER ELEVEN

THE GIRL SHRANK further back into the shadows as she was approached and Ryan slowed his pace to let Evie get there first. It had to be far less intimidating to have someone female and petite coming towards you than a large, strange male. Who knew what kind of history this girl had with men?

Nobody could see Evie's smile and the genuine warmth in her eyes and not trust her, surely? Even her voice, when she spoke, was as gentle as the tone she used with miserable babies.

'It's okay,' Evie was saying. 'It's really okay...we just want to help.'

The girl said nothing, just stared at Evie.

'You must be freezing.' Evie was pulling off the warm jacket she was wearing. 'Here...put this on.' She stepped forward and wrapped the jacket around the girl's shoulders as if it was the most natural thing in the world to do. Like a mother with a toddler who was crying from the cold. 'Are you hungry?'

Ryan doubted the girl was even aware of what she was revealing by the way she licked her lips.

'Come with us?' Evie hadn't let go of the girl's

shoulders after she had placed the jacket. 'There's a little café just inside the main doors of the hospital and they make the best macaroni cheese in the world.'

The girl shook her head, pulling away from Evie's grasp.

'No,' she whispered. 'I can't go in there...'

'Why not, hon?'

'I'm... I'm not supposed to be here. I'll get into trouble...'

'No, you won't.' Ryan spoke for the first time and smiled gently as the girl's startled gaze flew to his face. 'I promise, okay? And you know what?'

The silence lasted a heartbeat, and then another but the girl hadn't looked away.

'What?'

'I *always* keep my promises. I'm famous for it.'

A tiny huff of sound that could have been amusement came from the girl.

'It's true,' Evie added. 'This is Ryan. And I'm Evie...'

'I know who you are.' The girl hunched into the shelter of Evie's jacket. 'I saw you, that night...'

It was Evie's gaze that caught Ryan's now. A fleeting glance that communicated so much. They had to be right. This was Grace's mother and she'd been watching from not far away the night they had found the baby.

'What's your name?' Evie asked quietly.

'Um...' The response was reluctant. 'Lauren.'

Ryan edged a little closer. 'Hi, Lauren. It's good to meet you. Did you come back today because you want to know how...how your baby is?'

Lauren's chin was almost touching her chest. 'I saw

you on the telly. Talking about the operation she had to have on her heart but…but I haven't heard anything since then and I thought… I thought maybe she's… dead?'

'Oh, no…' Evie didn't hesitate. She closed the gap between herself and Lauren and wrapped her arms around the girl. 'No, hon. She's very much alive and doing so well. And she's the most beautiful baby. Just gorgeous… I love her to bits. We all do.'

Lauren burst into tears, her head on Evie's shoulder.

'So…you'll look after her?' she said between her sobs. 'You can adopt her?'

'It's not quite that simple,' Ryan said carefully. 'But we'll do whatever we can to help, okay?'

Lauren pulled away from Evie but staggered slightly. She might have fallen except that Ryan caught her.

'When did you last have something to eat?' he asked.

'I… I can't remember.'

'Come with us,' he said. 'Nobody else needs to know who you are at the moment and we can find a quiet corner where nobody's going to notice. Please let us give you something to eat and drink before you collapse and we have to take you to an emergency department.'

'You won't tell on me? Or call the police?'

'We won't do anything that you don't agree to,' Ryan told her. 'But we can't just let you disappear into the night when you're like this. Hey…if anyone asks, we can tell them you're Evie's sister, okay? She's got a sister who's about your age.'

Lauren turned to Evie. 'Really? What's her name?'

'Stella.'

'How old is she?'

'Fourteen. Nearly fifteen.' Evie had her arm around Lauren's shoulder and they'd started walking towards the hospital entrance near the ambulance bay.

'I'm sixteen.'

'And you're living rough? Oh, hon...'

They didn't ask any more questions until they had Lauren sitting in the farthest corner of the café. Ryan sat opposite Lauren, as if shielding her from being seen by anyone else who came into the café.

Evie realised that it had probably been a conscious choice. Like the way he'd hung back outside to let her be the one to talk to Lauren first. He was instinctively protective, wasn't he? Gentle.

She loved that about him.

Lauren had a big plate of macaroni cheese in front of her and a mug of hot chocolate and she was eating as if she hadn't seen a proper meal in a very long time.

'I think you're amazing,' Evie finally said.

Lauren froze, her fork halfway to her mouth. 'What? Why did you say that?'

'I haven't had a baby,' Evie continued quietly, 'but I've seen and read enough to know how hard it can be. How painful. How terrifying it would be to do something like that all alone. *Were* you all alone?'

Lauren nodded. Her eyes filled with tears that escaped to roll down her cheeks. Ryan handed her a serviette.

'So that's what makes you amazing. You did that, all by yourself. And not only that, you chose a place to leave Gracie where you knew that she would be found and looked after.'

Lauren gasped. *'Gracie?'*

'We needed to give her a name,' Evie said. 'And… and Grace was my mum's name. She died, a long time ago now, but I still miss her. I think she would love that your baby has borrowed her name for a while.' She paused for a moment. 'Have you still got your mum, Lauren?'

The girl shook her head, her face scrunching into lines of distress. 'She's still alive,' she muttered. 'But she kicked me out a long time ago. She reckoned her boyfriend fancied me more than her…and…and that I was leading him on.'

Evie noticed the way Ryan's eyes darkened. Was it bringing back painful memories for him? Of a child who had been rejected by their mother and felt unloved and unwanted? She'd never seen him look quite this serious. Upset, even.

Because he was feeling connected?

Emotionally involved?

Wow…was it only a few short weeks ago that she'd seen this man focused only on clinical information about someone and able to keep himself shut off from any kind of involvement that might affect his professional judgement or performance?

He cleared his throat. 'It wasn't… Um… Was he the father of your baby, Lauren?'

She shook her head. 'No… I was long gone by the time I got pregnant. I was living in a squat house. It was just some boy. I thought… I thought he cared about me but he took off when he found out about the baby.'

'Did you see a doctor at all when you were pregnant?'

Again, Lauren shook her head. 'I was scared they'd take me home. That there'd be trouble with the police and things would get even worse.'

'They don't have to be,' Evie said. 'There are lots of people out there who just want to help someone like you, Lauren. If you wanted to keep your baby, they would make it possible.'

'No...' Lauren shoved her chair back but, being in the corner with Evie on one side and Ryan opposite, there was nowhere for her to go. 'I don't. I *can't...* I can't even look after myself properly. I just want... I just want her to have a good home. With people who will love her.' Her eyes were desperate as she looked from Evie to Ryan and back again. 'People like *you...*'

'We can help you to find a family for Grace, if it's what you really want,' Evie told her gently. 'But, to make it happen, we need *your* help, too. You'll need to talk to people from Social Services. Sign things, I expect. And they'll want to make sure it is what you *really* want.'

'It is...'

'So, would you feel ready to tell them that?'

'What about the police?'

'They'll need to know,' Ryan said, 'because they've been looking for you. Everybody's been worried about you as well as Grace. But you won't get into trouble.'

Lauren's lips were trembling. 'You promise?'

Ryan smiled. 'I promise.' He glanced at Evie. 'Can we find somewhere private? And let people know?'

He lowered his voice. 'You might want to find out if Theo's still in the hospital.'

'You won't leave me, will you?' Lauren looked terrified. 'I don't want to talk to anyone if you're not here.'

'We're not going anywhere,' Ryan promised.

It was nearly an hour later that anything official started happening.

They had chosen one of the family rooms attached to the ICU to gather the necessary personnel, possibly because it was such familiar territory for Evie or maybe because it was close to where the most important person in this drama was. Baby Grace.

Theo Hawkwood was there. Lauren had been given a thorough medical check-up and a policewoman had come to take Lauren's statement and reassure her that no charges were going to be laid. Now they were talking to Sandra, from Social Services, and she was also treating Lauren very kindly.

'We're going to find somewhere for you to live,' she said. 'And help if you want to go back to school.'

Lauren shook her head. 'I sucked at school. I'm really stupid.'

Ryan leaned forward in his chair. 'That's not true, Lauren.'

He caught her gaze as she lifted her head and held it. He could see intelligence in those brown eyes but he could see that any hope had been extinguished because she had been totally failed by people around her. That it was her own mother who was most responsible made his heart ache in a way it hadn't since he had been a child himself. He knew he could shut those feelings away. Step back and look at the big picture in a way that was possibly going to be more useful in finding a way forward for this lost teenager but…he didn't want to.

That would be a form of rejection as well, wouldn't it?

'You're smart,' he told her quietly. 'You need to believe that, sweetheart. Yes, you need some help and I know it's hard to ask for that but if you can accept it and start believing in yourself, you'll find out who you really are. You'll find out that you can do whatever might be your dream.' He reached out to touch the back of her hand with his fingertips. 'Do you have a dream, Lauren?'

The young girl pushed the lank strands of her hair away from her face as she turned her head to give Evie a shy glance.

'I'd like to be a nurse,' she whispered. 'Like Evie…'

Evie smiled at her. 'I'm not a nurse yet,' she said. 'But I'm going to be. Soon, I hope. I had to decide what my dream was, too, and, you know what?'

'What?'

'It was something Ryan said that made me believe it was possible and…and I *really* believe it now. You should, too. He's right about lots of things.'

Evie glanced at him then, and Ryan got an odd lump in his throat that made it difficult to swallow. That look told him that she *did* believe in him. That she trusted him completely. There was something more in her eyes, as well. Something so warm and deep that the lump got so big it was hard to even get a breath around it.

'If you want to be a nurse,' Sandra said, 'you will need to go back to school, Lauren. You'll need to work hard to catch up on everything you've missed and get the grades that would get you into the training programme. But, like Ryan said, it *is* possible. I can help you.'

'Oh… I'd really like that.' Lauren's eyes were swimming with tears. 'I will work hard, I promise.'

'Okay. We'll work on that very soon but, right now, we need to talk about your baby and what's going to happen.'

'I can't keep her,' Lauren said. 'I really can't. I just came back here because I had to know that she was okay…'

Ryan heard Evie pull in a breath. 'Would you like to see her?' she asked Lauren softly, and Sandra nodded in the silence that followed.

'It might help,' she said to Lauren. 'It might be the best way to know if giving her up for adoption is what you really want.'

'I'll go and get her,' Evie said. 'And bring her in here. You can see her. You can hold her, if you want to. She loves cuddles.'

Maybe it was only Ryan who could hear the catch in Evie's voice. Or notice the way she brushed a fingertip beneath her eyes as she headed out of the room. While she was gone, Sandra organised her paperwork.

'It's your signature we're going need here, Dr Hawkwood. And here…' She showed Theo the spaces. 'I'll leave copies with you so that you can have them checked by your legal team if necessary. Hope Hospital has had guardianship and it was you who signed the original paperwork to take on the responsibility. We will need your signed agreement that you're hand-ing over that care when the time comes for Grace to go to her foster family. She's well enough for discharge now, yes?'

Evie came back into the room with the small bundle in her arms as both Ryan and Theo confirmed that Grace was well enough to be discharged. She went to stand beside Lauren, tilting the bundle so that Grace's little face was visible.

'Oh...' Lauren stared at her baby. 'She's...beautiful.'

Evie's smile wobbled a little. 'I know... I've seen so many babies in here but I'm quite sure that Gracie is by far the most beautiful. She's just gorgeous. And so brave... It was a huge operation that was needed to fix her heart but look at her now. She's just a normal, happy little baby.'

Lauren sucked in a deep breath. 'Can I...can I hold her?'

'Of course.' Evie transferred the bundle and showed Lauren how to hold her baby securely.

'Would you like a photograph?' Sandra asked.

Lauren nodded. She didn't smile, however. Or even look up as Sandra took some photographs with her phone. She was too intent on looking at the baby she was holding.

For a long time then they all simply sat in silence.

Ryan watched Lauren and the way she was looking at Grace as if she was trying to memorise every tiny feature. And then he watched Evie watching Lauren and he could see how hard this was for Evie. Her face was pale and there were lines of stress around her eyes. This was the first real step towards losing Grace from her life. Maybe Lauren would decide she wanted to keep her baby but, if she didn't, Sandra would have to start the procedure to place her into foster care, ready for adoption. Hope Hospital was no longer the official guardian of a sick, abandoned baby.

It was Grace who broke the silence by starting to cry. Lauren looked alarmed and looked to Evie for assistance. Evie gathered the baby back into her own arms and bent her head to kiss Grace. Almost immediately, the baby's cries lessened and within a very short space of time she was asleep again. Ryan watched the process and remembered telling Evie that she was a born mother. Surely everyone in the room could feel the love she had for this baby.

Sandra smiled at Lauren. 'How do you feel about things now, love?'

The teenager twisted her hands together. 'She's beautiful,' she said slowly, 'but…it doesn't feel like she's mine, you know? And I know that I can't give her the kind of life that somebody else could. A couple like Evie…and Ryan.'

Ryan swallowed hard. 'We're not a couple, Lauren.'

'What? But I thought…' Confused, Lauren looked from Ryan back to Evie and then she dropped her head. 'Sorry…'

'There are lots of people out there,' Sandra put in, 'including single carers, who would welcome a baby like Grace. But we're going to give you a few days to think about it, okay? I'm going to take you to a safe house now and we'll make arrangements for more permanent accommodation. If you want, you can come back and visit Grace again.'

But Lauren shook her head. 'I don't need to,' she said. 'But...there is something I'd like to do.'

'What's that?'

Lauren had her hands at the back of her neck. 'I'd like to give her this,' she said. 'It's a necklace that my gran gave me when I was little. Before she died...'

It was a small gold heart on a chain that she held up to Evie. 'Can you look after it?' she asked. 'And make sure it stays with her?'

Evie nodded but her swift, almost startled, glance at Ryan made him suddenly remember something that he should have remembered a long time ago. He had collected Evie's broken necklace when he'd picked up his tuxedo from the drycleaner's the day they'd gone to the charity ball. He had taken it to a jeweller's shop to get it repaired but, somehow, he hadn't found the time to go back and collect it.

He would do that. Tomorrow.

Right now, though, he was more worried about how Evie was going to cope with the beginning of the end of her time with baby Grace.

Her heart had to be breaking into small pieces.

He was still feeling that ache himself and it had suddenly got more fierce. As though *his* heart was trying to break as well.

CHAPTER TWELVE

THE PAIN WOULD go away eventually.

Wouldn't it?

How could his life have changed so much in such a short space of time? It had happened in a split second, really. Probably in that moment when Evie had been sent sprawling by his inebriated companion—before he'd even set foot in Hope Hospital for the very first time. And, if not then, it had certainly been in that moment of discovering the abandoned baby.

Ryan hunched into his coat as he strode through the gates of the hospital the next morning. A sideways glance reminded him that he couldn't even see the staff car park or the rubbish bins from this point in the grounds but that didn't stop the memories surfacing with complete clarity.

He had had no idea how symbolic that incident of Evie being knocked over had been. There was...good grief, what was her name again? Oh, yeah... Tiffany. Just the kind of woman he'd always been attracted to. Great looking, polished and only interested in a good time for however long it lasted. And there was her polar opposite—Evie, in those plain clothes and wearing no make-up and just so...*real.*

Ryan remembered the shock of discovering that she was a receptionist and not a nurse as he walked through the main doors of Hope Hospital and how that had sparked his curiosity about her. How that curiosity had morphed into feeling injustice on her behalf that she had had to sacrifice so much of her life for others. That she had learned to put herself down and hide in the background. That others were always more important and she did whatever was needed to try and make them happy, giving up her career for her family, her free time for baby Grace, even her best efforts for Theo Hawkwood and any other people here that needed her help.

It was no wonder that he'd seen that she needed things for herself. Like encouragement to follow her dream of becoming a nurse. And having a night out just so that she could shine and enjoy herself. Pushing the button of the elevators made him remember taking her up in the elevator of his apartment block after that extraordinary night of the charity ball. The sheer force of the desire that he hadn't been able to withstand. The discovery of what it was actually like to make love to a woman and not simply use sex as a form of physical release.

That was the source of this pain, that was for sure.

He loved Evie Cooper.

Maybe right from the start, when he'd reached down to help her up from the ground. No...maybe what had broken that barrier had been when he'd seen her hold-

ing Grace and he'd been swamped with that longing
that he couldn't really name. Or didn't want to. The
longing to be held like that himself. To be loved. To
be part of a family.

But it was one thing to know what it was that he
yearned for. Quite another to trust that it was possible.
He'd thought that maybe he was incapable of feeling an
emotional involvement like this but he'd proved himself wrong. Now he was grappling with the realisation that perhaps what he was incapable of was trust.
He'd protected himself for ever by simply not allowing
those feelings to take hold and now he'd lost that protective shield, but he was still a long way away from
being able to follow those feelings and open himself
up to the pain of loss. This pain of wanting something
so badly and knowing he couldn't try to keep what he
wanted was far less than it would be if it was given to
him and then taken away.

How stupid had it been to go and look at that house
with Evie? It had only made things so much worse.
Made him imagine having a Sunday lunch with her in
that village pub. Imagine sharing that house with her.
No wonder he'd felt that much closer to her when he'd
been watching her struggling with the knowledge that
Grace was going to vanish from her life very soon.

His pager sounded before he'd reached his office.
The paediatric cardiology team needed a consult, ur-
gently, in one of the wards. Ryan dumped his coat and
briefcase in his office and headed straight to the ward,
realising with relief that any memories were fading into
oblivion. Thankfully, that ache in his chest was abat-
ing just as effectively.

* * *

It was the same parking space.

How ironic was that?

Evie shut off the engine of her car but, for the longest time, she couldn't summon the motivation to open the door and head into work.

She also needed the motivation to pull herself together and find the focus that would render any broken fantasy no more than a part of the past. Something that she could learn from and then move on. She'd done it before. She'd recovered from her first heartbreak and she'd successfully avoided any danger of that happening again for years and years and years.

Ryan had been everything she had been determined to avoid. A doctor. A playboy. Someone unable to make a commitment and therefore someone that couldn't be trusted. So what the hell had happened here, just a few weeks ago?

Whatever it was, it had happened in a matter of seconds—as shockingly as that impact with the asphalt of this car park had been that night.

Even now, her mind could summon up the smell of his aftershave as he'd bent down to help her up. Except that it hadn't been aftershave, had it? She knew now that that scent was simply his own. It had been just another astonishing revelation that night when he'd made love to her. She had even been able to taste it on his skin...

Reaching for the door handle made Evie aware of the muscles in her arm and that was enough for her traitorous brain to remind her of the strength in Ryan's arm as he'd helped her to her feet after that fall. Of that intense stare he'd subjected her to. The kind of look that nobody who actually intended keeping their distance from someone else would be capable of delivering.

He might think he shut himself off from being involved with others, but he didn't. He was deeply involved with everything he did—he'd just learned to hide it, even from himself. Like yesterday, when they'd been with Lauren as she'd made the decision to give her baby up for adoption. She could see that it was affecting him. She could also see that he wasn't about to admit it. Or allow it to change his life in any way.

With a sigh, Evie hauled herself from the car and set off towards the back entrance of the hospital. The thought that she would have time to visit Grace before she started work failed to bring any comfort because she knew the clock was ticking and time was so limited and...and she was going to miss Grace *so* much. This was her own fault. She had become far too involved. Too attached.

Holding Grace a short time later made it all so much harder.

Yes, she'd become far too attached to this baby.

And she had done exactly the same thing with Ryan.

How stupid had it been to fall in love with him?

Stroking Grace's silky head made her remember that first night. The way his hand had cradled this head so gently when he'd been trying to soothe her enough to be able to listen to her heart.

The way he'd made Evie feel so special by telling her that he'd been waiting for her in the car park to give her back the necklace. Her stomach actually seemed to twist as she remembered the force of the physical attraction that had kicked in at that point. Birth pains of the fantasy that had grown wings and reached its climax on that magical night of the ball.

That first kiss…

The slide of her dress slipping off to reveal her body and the admiration in Ryan's eyes as he'd swept her off her feet and into his bed.

But she'd been holding this baby again when that fantasy had shattered. When he'd snapped at her and told her that Grace wasn't a toy.

It still hurt.

She had been prepared to trust again and that trust had been broken.

But she had dealt with worse. The death of her mother put anything else into perspective and look how far she'd come. And what she had to look forward to. The letter had been waiting for her when she got home yesterday. She had been accepted back into her nursing training and could start in the new year.

A new year. A new career. A new life.

It should all be so exciting. So why did that big, fat tear drop from her face and land on Grace's head?

'So it's end-stage heart failure. Terminal, unless we can pull something out of the hat very soon.'

Ryan nodded. The grim face of the cardiologist he was speaking with said it all. This child's condition was critical and calling him in was simply the last possible option.

'The parents must know how serious this is?'

'That's why they've brought him here. He's been

on the waiting list for a heart transplant but they've run out of time.'

'There's nothing we can do that could guarantee giving him enough time. Even using an intra-aortic balloon pump as a bridge to surgery can only buy a limited amount of time.'

'I know. But it *is* something we can do. That you could do, anyway. If nothing else, his parents will know that everything possible has been done for their son. And who knows? Maybe a miracle will happen and a transplant will become available.'

It was moments like this that never failed to remind Ryan of his baby brother. Jack's death had always been there somewhere in the back of his mind and it was probably what had steered Ryan into this career as much as any fascination with such complex surgeries. Like Jack, the little boy that had been rushed in early this morning had such major abnormalities with his heart that no surgical procedure could fix it. Decades ago, the possibility of a heart transplant or an intra-aortic balloon pump would probably not have been a consideration but if it had been, he could be sure that his mother would have clung to any hope it might provide.

He was silent for a long moment and then he nodded slowly.

'Okay. I'm prepared to try but I need to speak to his parents first. They need to understand what a long shot this really is.'

'Of course. Come with me... We've got them in one of our private rooms on the cardiology ward.'

What neither of these doctors expected was to walk

into the scene of a cardiac arrest and resuscitation attempt.

'Can someone take over compressions, please? We need to intubate.'

Ryan stepped forward without hesitation. His hand looked far too big on the small chest and he had to control the pressure he was using carefully so as not to cause damage to fragile ribs and the organs beneath them. And his compressions needed to be rapid, between a hundred and a hundred and twenty per minute.

The doctor in charge of the crash team that had been summoned was administering adrenaline. The pads for the defibrillator were already in place.

'Stand clear. Charging...'

Ryan lifted his hand. 'Clear.'

As the whine of the electrical charge increased intensity before changing to a strident beep, he took a swift glance over his shoulder. As he'd feared, the parents of this child were in the room. Clinging to each other and looking absolutely terrified.

He started the compressions as soon as the shock had been delivered. Another two minutes and their tiny patient had been intubated and was on continuous oxygen instead of needing to be bag-masked. Another shock, another cycle of drugs and another two minutes of chest compressions.

They kept the attempt going for more than thirty minutes but glances were already being exchanged between the medical staff. They all knew that this was hopeless but every member of the team had to be in agreement before a halt was called. Finally, those glances were accompanied by subtle nods and they stood back. Someone shut off the alarm sounding on the defibrillator.

The parents had been warned that this was coming by a nurse who'd stayed by their side. They had been able to witness that everything possible had been done for their little boy but this silence in the wake of the failed attempt was dreadful. It was Ryan who broke it.

'I'm so sorry,' he said.

The heartbroken wail from the child's mother was truly awful. Her husband wrapped her tightly into his arms and rocked her, tears streaming down his own face.

Something was breaking inside Ryan at that moment. This must have been how his own mother had felt when she'd lost Jack but she hadn't had his father there to support her. How dreadful must that have been? The only family she'd had apart from Jack had been another young child who couldn't understand what was happening and, even if he had, he hadn't been allowed close enough to offer any kind of comfort.

Had his mother shut down her ability to feel anything after that because it was a means of survival for her? Had she inadvertently taught him the skills he'd needed to keep his own distance?

He could forgive her, he realised.

He could understand.

Maybe there would even come a time when he could tell her that.

He had to leave the room at that point because the feeling that something was breaking was escalating.

Ryan needed to be alone.

But he couldn't be alone, either. Because he knew

that whatever was happening to him emotionally was going to explode and he'd never felt more vulnerable in his life. He had no idea how to handle such over-whelming emotions.

Who could he trust to see him like this and under-stand? Someone who might even be able to help?

There was only one person. There could only ever be one person.

He had to find Evie.

She saw Ryan the moment he stepped out of the el-evator.

Because she'd looked up from behind her desk. As if she'd felt his presence even as the doors of the el-evator slid open?

With the same instinct, she knew that something was wrong.

Terribly wrong.

She pushed her chair back so fast it tipped over, but she didn't bother to pick it up. She went straight to-wards Ryan and the expression in his eyes frightened her. She held out her hand and, when he took it, she led him into the nearest family room, shut the door behind them and locked it.

Ryan stepped slowly towards a couch and sank down onto it.

Evie sat down beside him. She didn't know what to ask to try and find out what the matter was but she was here for him. Whatever it was, she wasn't going anywhere.

Ryan's words, when he finally spoke, were broken. Agonised.

'He died, Evie. Before I could even try and help him...' Ryan buried his face in his hands so it was harder to hear the muffled words. 'He was just a baby and...and his mother was there...'

The sound of the broken sob was shocking.

Heartbreaking.

Evie wrapped her arms around Ryan's shaking shoulders. Pulled his head down so that she could cradle it. Pressed her own head against his. She was crying, too. Aching for the pain that Ryan was experiencing. Knowing that a dam had been breached and that it had to be terrifying for him to be feeling this much and be unable to control it the way he always had.

She had no idea how long they sat there. She didn't even care that she'd deserted her post. Michelle would just have to cope.

Ryan's sobs faded and stopped but the only movement he made was to put his arms around Evie so that now they were holding each other.

'I'm sorry,' he murmured.

'What for? Caring?' Evie pressed a kiss to that tousled, streaky hair. 'It's who you are, Ryan. You don't ever have to hide that from me.'

'I've never cried.' Ryan's breath came out in a sigh. 'Not when I'm awake, anyway. Not since I was a kid...'

'That's a lot of tears that have been bottled up, then.' Evie tilted her head to try and see his face. 'Does it feel better to have let some of them go?'

Ryan sat up but he didn't let go of Evie. He pulled her close so that she was tucked against his shoulder.

'I think it does.' He gave an enormous sniff. 'But I don't intend to make a habit of it, you know.'

'Of course not.'

'It was just that sometimes…when I meet a patient who's terminal, it makes me think of my brother. And today… I could see how it must have been for my mum. How unbearable it must have been.'

Evie nodded. 'Life can seem unbearable sometimes. There's only one thing that can help.'

Ryan caught her gaze and held it.

'I knew *you'd* be able to help. There was no one else…'

'That's because I can give you what you need. What you've always needed.' Her lips were trembling too much to let her smile properly. 'Love,' she added in a whisper. 'I love you, Ryan.'

'I know…' He opened his mouth to say more but then closed it again.

Had he been going to say that he loved her, too?

Instead, he eased out of her arms, put a hand on each side of Evie's head and kissed her.

A long, slow, exquisitely tender kiss.

'I have to go,' he said. 'I'm due in Theatre.'

'Will you be okay?'

He nodded. 'I can do this. I've always been able to do this. Although maybe not quite like this…'

'Because now it's different…?'

Ryan smiled at her. 'It is. But, you know what?'

'What?'

'I think it's better. Or it will be, when I've got my head around it properly.' He glanced at his watch and then back at Evie as he headed for the door and unlocked it. 'There's something I need to do after work, too, but will you meet me? At six o'clock?'

'Sure. Where?'

Ryan turned his head, one eyebrow raised as he smiled again. 'You know where...'

And then he was gone. Walking tall again. Nobody would ever know what had happened between them in this room.

Nobody ever would. It was their secret. A real smile curved Evie's lips, then. She was pretty sure she knew where Ryan wanted to meet her.

It wasn't exactly a romantic rendezvous to have chosen, out by the bank of huge rubbish bins at the back of Hope Hospital, but Ryan was barely aware of the background as he walked towards them.

He could only see Evie standing there and that was the most beautiful sight in the world. He could feel his smile growing as he strode closer.

'You guessed.'

'Well, it was a toss up between here and where I fell over in the car park but I figured that this was the spot that the most important thing happened for both of us.'

Even as Ryan opened his arms to pull her into them, Evie raised hers to wrap them around his neck. It was too easy to lift her completely off her feet as he kissed her. Then he set her down gently. And kissed her again.

'I need to apologise,' he murmured, his lips still close enough to feel hers.

'What for? Kissing me?'

He laughed. 'No... I'm never going to apologise for that.' In fact, he had to kiss her again.

'What for, then? Not about what happened today?'

Ryan shook his head. 'No. I'm not sorry about that

either. You've taught me to feel again, Evie, but...way more than that. I know that I can keep doing that...' He had to swallow the lump in his throat. 'As long as I can keep doing it with you. I love you, Evie. I think I have from the moment I first saw you.'

This time, it was Evie who kissed him, although he had to bend his head to let it happen, even when she was standing on tiptoes. How could so many wonderful things be wrapped up in such a small, human parcel?

'I love you, too, Ryan,' she said, quite a long time later. 'But... I still don't get what you're apologising for.'

'Oh... I almost forgot. *Again*.' Ryan fished in his pocket and took out a small package. 'It's your necklace. I know you said you didn't want me to get it fixed for you but I didn't want to give it back broken. I know how special it is to you.'

Evie's eyes were shining. 'I thought it might have been lost for ever.' She held the necklace in her hand. 'It's lovely, isn't it? Dad bought it for Mum for a wedding anniversary. He said that a topaz had to be her stone because it was the same colour as her eyes. I think it was the most romantic thing he ever did for her and it's even more special to me because I was the only one of their children who inherited exactly the same coloured eyes.'

Ryan couldn't look away from those eyes right now.

'Could you help me put it back on? My fingers are so cold I don't think they're working any more.'

'Mine are frozen, too. See?' Ryan touched the back of Evie's neck and she squeaked. 'Let's go somewhere a bit warmer.'

'Home?'

'Not just yet. Have you been to see Grace today?'

'Not since this morning. I didn't want to be late meeting you after work.'

'Let's go and see her now. Together.'

By the time Evie had changed into scrubs so that she could go into the NICU, her fingers had warmed up enough to manage the clasp on her necklace but she still had it dangling from her hand as she emerged from the changing rooms to find Ryan waiting for her.

He took it from her hand without a word. Maybe he understood that she wanted him to put it on for her. Or perhaps that was what he'd wanted as well. She was tempted to slip her hand into his as they walked into the unit together but that would hardly be professional, would it, and Evie was quite confident that there would be plenty of handholding in the near future.

And more. So much more…

It was Ryan who lifted Grace from her crib and put her into Evie's arms. Susie went past as they settled into their chairs and she made a sympathetic face.

'It's going to be sad to see her go, isn't it?'

Evie blinked hard. She cuddled Grace closer and tried to focus on something positive. That this baby was healthy enough to be discharged from hospital. That she was here with Ryan.

That he loved her. That *she* loved him…

And that he cared so much about this tiny patient of his, as well. The way he reached out now and stroked her hair so gently just melted her heart all over again.

'What if we didn't have to see her go?'

His words were so quiet Evie thought she might have imagined them but then he lifted his gaze to catch hers.

'What if we could be allowed to adopt her? That's what Lauren wanted and…and maybe she was right.'

'But…'

How could it have been such a blink of time since they'd been in that room with Lauren and Theo and Sandra. When Ryan himself had explained that they weren't actually a couple?

'But how could we? Sandra said there would be people out there who would want her. We're not even…'

'Married?'

Evie could feel her cheeks going pink. 'I was going to say engaged.' Oh, help…it was too soon to be thinking that far ahead. 'Or official, anyway.'

'We could do something about that.' Ryan leaned back in his chair. He was taking something from the pocket on his scrubs tunic. 'The thing is…when I went to the jeweller's today to collect your necklace, I found something else…'

He was holding a tiny velvet box and he flipped the lid open.

'It was such a perfect match,' he said with a smile. 'And the jeweller said that it was so different he hadn't been sure anyone would want it. It felt like it was meant to be.'

The ring in the box was a perfect match to her mother's necklace. A sparkling diamond that was surrounded by tiny stones that were the same golden brown as the topaz that was now back where it belonged, around Evie's neck.

'You don't have to wear it on your left hand,' Ryan

said softly. 'Or not yet, anyway. I know this is probably way too soon. That you might need time to get used to the idea but...'

To Evie's astonishment, Ryan was slipping from his chair. Onto one knee. From the corner of her eye she could see that people were watching. Susie and others had stopped in their tracks.

'But I love you, Evie,' Ryan continued. 'I've never felt like this before and I never want to stop. I told you I could never share your dreams but I was wrong. I want to share them. With *you*. Only ever with you.'

Evie didn't bother trying to blink away these new tears. She held out her hand. Her left hand.

'I don't need time,' she whispered. 'I love you, too. I want those dreams with you.'

The ring fitted perfectly.

Of course it did.

It was the perfect match for her precious necklace.

And they were the perfect match for each other. It was, indeed, meant to be.

It was just as well that this space had been built with the very best sound muffling materials because it meant that the soft clapping from everyone nearby didn't disturb their patients.

Except that Grace had woken up. She looked up at the woman who held her in her arms and at the man who was kissing her. And, for the very first time in her life, she smiled...

EPILOGUE

'I HOPE YOU'RE not thinking of *using* that stepladder for anything?'

Evie had to smile at the horrified look on Ryan's face. 'Our angel's in danger of falling off the tree. Look…'

Ryan put the guard back in place in front of the roaring fire that was warming the huge living area in this barn conversion that had become a much-loved home. Looking up, he spotted that the angel was hanging precariously by the edge of her wing.

'That's what happens when you let a two-year-old do the final decoration, I guess.' He was smiling but there was a frown line between his eyes as he firmly removed the small stepladder from Evie's hands.

Evie's smile widened. She'd taken a photo of Ryan holding Gracie up in his arms so that she could do the honours with the decoration she loved the most. Their adopted daughter had fallen in love with the angel so much, they had given her an early Christmas present of her own set of fluffy wings and it had been a mission for weeks now to persuade her to take them off when it was bedtime.

Ryan straightened and secured the decoration on the top of the tall tree, leaning carefully over the pile of gifts beneath the tree. Then he stood back to admire it, his arm around Evie.

'It's perfect,' Evie murmured.

Ryan bent his head to kiss her. 'It is.'

They both knew that they were talking about more than just a Christmas tree. One, brief, shared glance was an acknowledgement that, despite the ups and downs of life, what made it as perfect as possible was having the people that you loved to share it with. The pretty tree was simply a symbol of the time of year when you gathered those people together and celebrated the joy of family.

'I'm glad Kylie was here to help decorate it. I hope she's enjoying the sun right now.' Their nanny had gone home to Australia for Christmas.

'She'll be gutted when she hears about the snow. She said she's always wanted a white Christmas.'

'Maybe she'll be able to stay next year.'

'I hope so. We might need the extra help by then.' Ryan drew Evie closer with one arm, his other hand tracing a familiar route to the growing bump of her belly but his head turned a moment later. 'Where's our number one angel?'

'She won't come away from the window. She's got her nose pressed to the glass, waiting for everybody to arrive. She wants her uncle Bobby to help her build a snowman.'

'We've got that toboggan under the tree for her, too. That'll be fun.' Ryan picked up the stepladder. 'I'll just go and put this away before she sees it. Goodness only knows what ideas it would give our Gracie.'

'She's a daredevil, all right.' Evie followed Ryan through the kitchen to the butler's pantry. 'All those times I sat holding her in Intensive Care, I'd never have dreamed she'd be running around like this now. There was a baby I was looking after yesterday who's pretty sick and I told her mum about Gracie. That I knew how scary things were for her right now.'

'You're loving being back where you belong, aren't you? In NICU?'

'Couldn't love it any more. And now I'm a real nurse. I don't feel like a fraud when I put my scrubs on.'

'You were never a fraud. You were the secret weapon. Our baby whisperer.'

'I'm going to miss it all over again when this one arrives.' Evie put her hand on her belly, loving the kick she received in response.

'You'll be too busy to notice.' Ryan slotted the stepladder into the corner. 'Who else would have signed up to use their maternity leave to do a specialist postgrad paediatric nursing course?'

Evie just smiled. She opened the back door to let in their newest family member but promptly banished him to the utility room.

'Stay in here,' she ordered. 'Until those paws dry off a bit.'

'It's going to be chaos when he comes out, you do know that, don't you?'

Evie nodded, but she was smiling. 'Who knew that

he was going to grow up to be this bouncy? He was such a quiet baby a few months ago.'

'He and Gracie are kindred spirits.'

'True.'

'It's no wonder they love each other so much.'

They shared a glance that made them both smile. Their newest family member was the happiest and friendliest dog they'd ever seen but he was also the strangest-looking mix of breeds with ears that were too big and legs that were too short and hair that stuck out in all directions. It was probably why nobody else had chosen him at the rescue centre.

Why he'd been abandoned when he was only a few weeks old.

And why he was the perfect choice for this family. They'd shared a similar glance the day they'd gone to choose their first family pet. Not a word had been spoken but Ryan had known they were both thinking of exactly the same thing. Of the night they'd first met and had found an abandoned baby. And now that baby was the happiest two-year-old ever. The most loved, as well, by both her parents and her extended family.

Only Evie could have made this happen for him and Ryan knew he was the luckiest man on earth. It made him feel so misty-eyed right now that he had to blink hard and sniff. That was enough to distract him completely.

'Wow...something smells amazing in here.' Ryan paused beside the Aga to lift the lid of a saucepan. 'Mmm... I love bread sauce. Do you need any help with anything?'

'Not at the moment. I think it's all under control.

The turkey won't be done for a couple of hours but we'll need that time for presents.'

Ryan peeked under a tea towel covering an oven tray on the bench. 'Oh…my favourite. Pigs in blankets. Hey… I'm starving already.'

Evie laughed. 'You'll just have to wait. Let's go and find our daughter.'

They passed the dining table that they'd stayed up late last night to decorate and it looked as perfect as the tall tree under the beams of the living room, with its red tablecloth and the sparkling wine glasses and silverware that had been a wedding present from Evie's family.

'You and Gracie did a good job with that thing in the middle.'

'It's called a centrepiece. It's just as well you didn't see the mess of glitter when we were making it. Do you think I should light the candles now?'

'Not yet.' Ryan was aware of that unfamiliar beat of nervousness that had become increasingly frequent in the last few days. Not for what the mix of a toddler and lighted candles could produce, though.

He felt Evie's hand touch his arm and then squeeze it.

'It'll be okay. You'll see…'

He nodded. He was looking at the chairs around the table now. Counting them.

Four for Evie's family. Her dad, Peter, Stella and Bobby. One each for himself and Evie. A highchair for Grace.

And one extra.

'*Dadda... Mumma...*' There was a patter of small feet on the floor. '*Cars...*'

Grace was tugging at his hand but Evie was still holding his other arm and he needed a moment more to reassure himself that she was right. That what was about to happen really would be a good thing.

Evie stood on tiptoes and the roundness of her belly pressed against him as she leaned in to pull his head close enough to kiss.

'Happy Christmas,' she whispered. 'I love you...'

'Love you too...'

Evie's family trooped through the door. Her father pushed a pile of gifts into Ryan's arms so that he could scoop up Grace.

'How's my favourite granddaughter?'

'I'm a *angel*,' Grace shouted happily, wriggling free of the cuddle after bestowing and receiving an enthusiastic kiss.

'Of course you are.'

It was Bobby who heard the barking coming from the direction of the utility room.

'Can I let him out?' His voice was as loud as Grace's. 'I haven't seen him for ages.'

Ryan took a deep breath as he caught Evie's gaze. 'I think it's time, don't you?'

'Let the fun begin.'

They were all coming back with the dog, whose long tail was wagging hard enough to announce that he was ecstatic to see the rest of his extended family, when there was a knock at the door. Nobody but Ryan heard it.

'He's still the weirdest looking dog I've ever seen,' Bobby was saying. 'He hasn't grown into those ears.'

'He still needs a proper name,' Evie responded. 'How 'bout you take him into the living room and see who can come up with the best one.'

'Dog.' Grace was almost knocked over by a kiss from her much-loved companion and she shrieked with laughter as her grandfather lifted her to safety. 'His name's Dog. Put me *down*, Grandpa.'

Everybody was laughing except Ryan. He waited until the flow of people left him alone beside the door. And then he opened it.

'Hello, Mum…'

She looked so much older it made his heart break. Older and just as sad as ever. Or maybe not… As she stared up at him, Ryan thought he could see something new in her eyes.

Hope?

This had been Evie's idea. She had encouraged him to make contact with his mum again when he'd told her that he thought he understood things enough to forgive her. It had been a long process. She hadn't been ready to come to her son's wedding eighteen months ago but she had finally accepted this invitation to come for Christmas. Just dinner because she said she preferred to stay in a London hotel but it was a start.

And if anybody could teach his mother that it was worth opening her heart to the joy of being able to love and be loved, it was going to be his beloved wife. He could hear the sound of excited cries and laughter coming from the warm interior of the house. Such a contrast to the blast of cold air from the snow-covered courtyard in front of him.

Ryan smiled at his mother and held out his hand.

'Come in,' he said softly. 'Welcome to our family...'

* * * * *

LET'S TALK
Romance

For exclusive extracts, competitions
and special offers, find us online:

- **f** facebook.com/millsandboon
- **⊙** @millsandboonuk
- **𝕐** @millsandboon

Or get in touch on 0844 844 1351*

For all the latest titles coming soon,
visit millsandboon.co.uk/nextmonth

Want even more
ROMANCE?

Join our bookclub today!

'Mills & Boon books, the perfect way to escape for an hour or so.'

Miss W. Dyer

'Excellent service, promptly delivered and very good subscription choices.'

Miss A. Pearson

'You get fantastic special offers and the chance to get books before they hit the shops'

Mrs V. Hall

Visit millsandbook.co.uk/Bookclub and save on brand new books.

MILLS & BOON